TAKING CARE OF BUSINESS

"What business you got with Alfie Doolittle, Fargo?"

He kneed the Ovaro and started him walking slowly toward the three men. "My business with Alfie is my own. I don't tell my business to folks I don't know."

"Oh, yeah?"

Fargo tensed, anticipating a reaction from his foe. He got one.

Fat Man's gun hadn't even cleared leather before Fargo's Colt was out, cocked and aimed at his gut, which made a very large target. Fargo saw him swallow.

"I don't care to be drawn on for no reason either," Fargo said in a soft, deadly voice. "What the hell's your name?"

"No need to get huffy, Fargo," Fat Man said. "Clay Franklin just hired me to watch out for trouble."

"I'm not trouble. I'm Skye Fargo."

"The one means the other, from what I've heard."

Fargo pulled the hammer back on his Colt.

Fat Man swallowed again. "You can put the gun away. I'm not going to do nothing . . ."

Fargo didn't believe it for a minute. His every nerve was snapping. . . .

THE TRAILSMAN

#218

PECOS BELLE BRIGADE

by

Jon Sharpe

A SIGNET BOOK

SIGNET
Published by New American Library, a division of
Penguin Putnam Inc., 375 Hudson Street,
New York, New York 10014, U.S.A.
Penguin Books Ltd, 27 Wrights Lane,
London W8 5TZ, England
Penguin Books Australia Ltd,
Ringwood, Victoria, Australia
Penguin Books Canada Ltd, 10 Alcorn Avenue,
Toronto, Ontario, Canada M4V 3B2
Penguin Books (N.Z.) Ltd, 182–190 Wairau Road,
Auckland 10, New Zealand

Penguin Books Ltd, Registered Offices:
Harmondsworth, Middlesex, England

First published by Signet, an imprint of New American Library,
a division of Penguin Putnam Inc.

First Printing, December 1999
10 9 8 7 6 5 4 3 2 1
Copyright © Jon Sharpe, 1999
All rights reserved

The first chapter of this book originally appeared in *Dakota Deception*,
the two hundred seventeenth volume in this series.

Ⓙ REGISTERED TRADEMARK—MARCA REGISTRADA

Printed in the United States of America

The Trailsman

Beginnings . . . they bend the tree and they mark the man. Skye Fargo was born when he was eighteen. Terror was his midwife, vengeance his first cry. Killing spawned Skye Fargo, ruthless, cold-blooded murder. Out of the acrid smoke of gunpowder still hanging in the air, he rose, cried out a promise never forgotten.

The Trailsman they began to call him all across the West: searcher, scout, hunter, the man who could see where others only looked, his skills for hire but not his soul, the man who lived each day to the fullest, yet trailed each tomorrow. Skye Fargo, the Trailsman, and the seeker who could take the wildness of a land and the wanting of a woman and make them his own.

1861, New Mexico Territory—where the fiercest winds and the fastest guns are no match for a woman spurned. . . .

1

A bad wind blew from the north, shrieking across the desolate plains like a soul in torment and driving hard pellets of frozen snow before it. It seemed to be trying to dislodge a lone rider from his saddle.

The man was big, though, and strong. He was also tough as old whitleather and wise to the ways of both wind and man. He sat his big pinto stallion stubbornly, refusing to give in to the gale. He hunched over, attempting to give the forceful wind a smaller target. The man was Skye Fargo, and he planned on getting to Spanish Bend, wind or no wind, snow or no snow.

Sleet stung the few bare patches of skin it could find on Fargo's face. He'd tied his hat down with a woolen muffler, and had a bandanna pulled over his nose and mouth. Both were now frozen solid. Fargo was pretty cold himself, in spite of the heavy leggings and sheepskin-lined jacket he wore.

His hands, encased in thick gloves, felt like blocks of ice. At this point, he wasn't altogether sure he could pry them free from the reins gripped tightly in his fingers if he had to.

Before the snow began, Fargo had watched a herd of antelopes foraging for grass on the winter-bare plains. Now even those few scrubby bunches of withered grama grass were buried under piles of snow, and his mind's eye pictured the antelopes, discouraged, bent against the howling wind just as he was.

He'd wondered before how those poor creatures managed to live out here. Even when the weather was fair, the pickings were slim in southeastern New Mexico Territory. He'd have thought any animal with a brain would have sought greener pastures. Not the pronghorns. Tough customers, those antelopes. Fargo admired their grit. He preferred to think of them as courageous rather than brainless. Under the circumstances, he feared he himself might be the brainless one.

He slouched farther over the Ovaro's back and cursed himself when the horse stumbled on something neither of them could see for the snow covering it. Fargo was a little worried about the harsh weather, although both he and his horse had been through worse conditions together. Not often, however, and seldom in such barren country.

It was impossible to see where he was going, and it was impossible to judge directions, even though he possessed a well-deserved reputation as a brilliant frontiersman. For all he knew, in spite of his years as a trailblazer in the wilderness, he and the Ovaro might be traveling around in slow circles.

He pictured that in his mind's eye too: him and his horse, foundering around and around until the snow stopped. Or until they froze into solid chunks, thus providing sustenance for any hungry coyotes in the neighborhood. No buzzards, though. The buzzards were wintering in Mexico. Smart birds, those buzzards, Fargo thought.

The truly bad weather never lasted long in these parts. It did its dirty work fast and went away again. There were no nine-month winters in southeastern New Mexico Territory. Winters out here usually came in treacherous patches that snuck up on a man and attacked him when his back was turned.

Nevertheless, Fargo knew it had been foolhardy of him to set out across these bleak plains when he'd known good and well a winter storm was brewing, and that he'd never get all the way to Spanish Bend before it hit. The land in these parts was hard, even when a body could see it. When it was covered with snow, as it was now, a horse might break a leg in a prairie-dog hole, walk into any number of needle-spiked cacti, or blunder into a snow-buried mesquite or greasewood plant. Fargo assumed his horse had just done the latter.

He peered through windblown snow flurries at a steel gray sky, and cursed himself again. The bareness of these plains made the wind seem especially bitter. There was nothing to stop it except the occasional idiot who ventured outdoors when it blew. Today he was the idiot, and he didn't like knowing it.

The only reason he'd done such a damnfool thing was because he'd been so worried by Kitty's letter. Hell, he'd known Kitty O'Malley forever, and he was as fond of her as he was of anyone. He'd met her in San Antonio, but the letter had been posted from the little town of Spanish Bend where, so she'd written, she'd opened a saloon. He'd planned to pay Kitty a visit anyway, but he'd aimed to do it when the weather was better.

Now, however, according to her letter, Kitty was in trouble, and Fargo aimed to help her get out of it. Since the trouble sounded both serious and urgent, he'd left the security of Fort Sumner in spite of the huge black clouds piled up in the north, and a wind as sharp as knives. He'd done so, against all of his frontier knowledge and survival instincts, for the sake of an old and dear friend.

"We'll be all right, boy," he assured the Ovaro, hoping he was right. If he managed to get himself killed, so be it. It was the chance he took every day of his life. But if he got his horse killed, he was an ass. Skye Fargo would rather put himself in jeopardy than his trusted mount, but oftentimes, like now, it couldn't be helped.

The sleet had thickened, and snow began falling hard and fast, almost horizontally now, thanks to the wind. Fargo estimated it was blowing a good twenty-five or thirty miles an hour. Faster than a train could move, for the love of God. He looked up again, hoping to perceive any kind of a hint that the weather might break soon. There was none. They were in for it, with no respite in sight. Damn.

Fargo didn't know how long he'd been in the saddle, getting stiffer and colder and wondering how long he and his horse could last, when the smell of wood smoke permeated the freezing air and his stiff bandanna. Hardly daring to believe it, his eyes opening wide in surprise and hope, he sniffed again.

It was definitely smoke from a wood fire. Sweet Lord have mercy, maybe there was some kind of life out here after all. He'd thought he'd have to ride clear to Spanish Bend before he and the Ovaro could thaw out.

Cheered considerably, Fargo guided the pinto through the heavy drifts. He did so carefully, and not merely because of the foul weather. While he didn't fancy freezing to death, he also didn't fancy getting shot. It wasn't only the landscape out here that was rough. The people who lived on it were often even rougher. They had to be.

"There it is, boy."

Squinting through the white veil of falling snow, Fargo could barely make out the glowing smear of a candlelit window. Snow muffled the sound of the

Ovaro's hooves, but Fargo approached the window warily. A few yards farther along he distinguished a dark bump rising from the snow like a monster out of a childhood nightmare. Squinting harder, he thought he could make it out as one small, lonely structure. It was more of a cabin than a house, he decided after another few moments of scrutiny. Smoke poured from the cabin's chimney, and was absorbed into the gray sky.

"It's not much of a place."

That was all right with Fargo. Any billet at all would be welcome at this point. He hoped there would be a barn or some kind of shelter for the Ovaro.

Few trees grew out here on the high plains, and those that did were stunted and had been shaped into low-growing, contorted forms by the eternal wind. Fargo had nothing behind which to conceal himself as he neared the cabin. His senses on the alert, he took off his right glove, tried to flex his fingers a few times, and drew his Colt. He trusted that if there were unfriendly gunmen inside, they were huddled around a fire and not expecting visitors.

He slowly circled the cabin on the Ovaro, which had a hard go of it through the deep drifts. Fargo was searching for any signs that the cabin's inhabitants might be hostile. There weren't any. He did, however, find a tumbledown barn. He considered this a good omen, since it ensured his horse shelter from the storm. And him, too, if whoever was inside that cabin wouldn't let him in.

Since snow had covered any tracks that might have been left by other cattle entering or leaving the barn, Fargo dismounted. His legs sank in a drift up to his knees, and his march to the barn's door was slow and laborious. When he finally got there, he stood aside and pushed the door open. Its hinges screeched like seventeen untuned fiddles. Fargo winced at the noise, and flattened himself against the side of the barn.

After the squealing of hinges quieted, the only thing that greeted him was silence and cavernous darkness. The eerie stillness lasted for several seconds before it was broken by the loud braying of a mule.

Fargo had been prepared for a shower of bullets. He wouldn't have been surprised by a fist in the face. The mule's sudden, unexpected "hee-haw" made him jump nearly out of his skin.

Almost simultaneously, he heard a window being pushed open, and a woman calling, "Who's out there? Show yourself, or I'll shoot." Fargo decided luck was truly on his side today. He'd recognize that voice anywhere. It belonged to Kitty O'Malley.

Relieved, he called back, "It's me, Kitty. Skye Fargo."

"Skye! Oh, Skye! You came!"

She sounded as if she'd been crying, which was unlike Kitty, who was at least as tough as nails and generally as cheerful as a bird. He frowned, not bothering to holster his Colt. "You alone in there, Kitty?"

"Except for a friend of mine, Sally Brown. You don't know her. Oh, Skye, I've needed you so bad!"

Good God, she *was* crying. Fargo was appalled. "Be right there. Got to take care of my horse."

"Hurry. Please hurry, Skye." Kitty sniffled loudly and slammed the window shut.

Unsettled by Kitty's obvious distress, Fargo entered the barn, being careful in case anyone might be lurking inside. The only thing in the barn was the mule, though, and it brayed again.

The coast was clear, so he reholstered his Colt and slid his glove over his nearly frozen fingers. Lord, he'd be glad to get inside and sit beside that fire with Kitty.

She'd always been able to warm him up in the past in more ways than one. To bad she had a friend with her. On the other hand, maybe this Sally Brown character was as friendly as Kitty. He felt warmer already.

The Ovaro didn't mind companionship either, so the Trailsman had no compunction about stabling him next to the noise maker. There were even some oats in a barrel.

Fargo gave his horse a good meal and some water, brushed him down, spread a blanket over him, and headed out of the barn. The wind almost yanked the door out of his hand, but he was able to get it shut again with a struggle. The snow and the wind had worsened into a regular blizzard, and he was mortally glad he'd discovered the cabin, especially since it was Kitty's. He was also glad the sun, if it was there, hadn't set yet. It was already almost too dark to see, and it couldn't be much past noon. Come nighttime, it would be black as pitch outdoors and too dangerous to travel, even for him.

Before he'd reached the door, Kitty had flung it open and barreled outside and into his arms. She was as warm as toast against his frozen body.

She leaped back almost as soon as she touched him. Fargo was disappointed.

"Shoot, Skye, you're freezing."

"You're t—telling me." He walked stiff-legged into the room.

Kitty closed the door behind him. "Lord, Skye, you look like an icicle."

Fargo didn't suppose the cabin would feel awfully warm to anyone who wasn't half frozen, but the air inside seemed to envelop him like heat in an oven, and to him it was heaven. He started to shiver uncontrollably, even as his clothes began thawing and dripping water onto the floor.

Kitty took him by the hand and led him to the fireplace. "Here, Skye, let me get these wet things off you."

"Th—thanks." Kitty tugged and Fargo heaved, and between them they managed to relieve him of his hat and jacket, muffler, gloves, and scarf. He felt much freer after that.

"How long have you been holed up in here, Kitty?" He was pleased to note an abundance of wood, chopped and stacked neatly next to the fireplace.

"I guess this is the third or fourth day. I kind of lost count."

"You lost c—count?" How the hell can a body lose count of days? He was too cold to ask.

She hung his jacket over the mantel to dry and spread his muffler and bandanna nearby. "Thank God I got the wood chopped before the snow started."

"You chopped the wood?" He guessed he'd sounded a little too incredulous when Kitty glared at him.

"Who the hell else was going to chop it?"

Since Fargo had no answer, he offered none. He was still too cold to talk, anyway.

The cabin consisted of two rooms. There wasn't much furniture in this one, which appeared to be the main living quarters. What little furniture there was looked like it had been through too many winters already, but Skye Fargo wasn't one to complain. He was accustomed to sleeping under the stars in all kinds of weather. This cabin was luxurious by comparison, and it contained Kitty, thereby rendering it much more appealing than a solitary bed outside, even if the weather had been fine.

Another room with a ragged curtain tacked up and

drawn back over the doorway revealed a bed. It looked as if someone was sleeping in it.

When his jaw thawed enough to move, Fargo asked, "That your friend Sally in there?"

He'd considered it a reasonable, even a simple, question. He guessed it wasn't when Kitty, as levelheaded a female as Fargo had ever known in his life, burst into tears.

"Here, Kitty, honey, don't cry. What's the matter? Is Sally sick or something?"

Kitty flung herself at him for the second time that day. This time, since he was no longer an ambulatory icicle, she didn't jump away again. Fargo hugged her hard, enjoying the feel of her supple flesh warming him up.

"She's sick, all right," Kitty sobbed. "She's dying, Skye! She was already sick. And then they beat her up something awful, and now she's dying! And it's all my fault!" She wailed the last sentence.

"What? Who beat her up? How's it your fault? What happened?"

"Clay Franklin. That's what happened. He happened to all of us."

"Sit down, honey, and tell me about it."

"Let me fetch you some food, Skye. You look half starved as well as half frozen."

Since he indeed was both, he nodded gratefully. While Kitty fetched a bowl and scooped some stew out of a pot hung on a spit over the fire in the fireplace, Fargo removed his boots and socks and his leather leggings. Thanks to his coat and his leggings, his britches were almost dry.

His feet were still as cold as ice, though, so he moved over to the fireplace and sat on a bearskin laid out in front of it. He aimed his feet at the fire, took the bowl of stew Kitty handed him, and ate hungrily. Kitty sat herself in a chair near him.

After he'd swallowed two bites of stew, he said, "So, tell me all about it, Kitty. Your letter said there was big trouble in Spanish Bend. I thought the place was too small for big trouble."

"You don't know New Mexico Territory," Kitty said grimly. "The whole place is trouble."

Fargo nodded. He'd been here before. What with Apaches and Comanches and outlaws and the hard land and harder weather, there wasn't a lot of peace to be found in the area.

"Why'd you leave San Antonio?"

"I wanted to open my own place. It was cheaper to do it out here, and they needed me." In spite of the state she was in, she managed a Kitty-like grin for him.

He smiled back. "You still a workin' girl, Kitty?"

"I am. And I had a swell place, too. Alfie Doolittle— you remember Alfie?"

"Sure do."

"Alfie said he'd help me."

Fargo grinned again. How could anybody ever forget Alfie? A wizened little man, Alfie had looked as old as the hills for as long as Fargo had known him, which was about as long as he'd known Kitty.

According to what Kitty had told Fargo a long time ago, she and Alfie weren't related by blood, but by affection. Alfie had played piano and tended bar in the first saloon Kitty'd ever entered, and they'd stuck together like fleas on a hound dog ever since.

As near as Fargo could tell, Alfie had never enjoyed Kitty's sexual favors. Rather, he acted as her surrogate father. Except that he didn't seem to mind that his surrogate daughter bedded other men for a living. Fargo wasn't judgmental by nature, and he didn't fault Alfie's tolerance.

"So you opened your own place in Spanish Bend with Alfie?"

Kitty nodded. "Alfie and me went in together in the business. I hired the girls and kept the books and Alfie played piano, tended bar, and acted as bouncer."

"Alfie acted as bouncer?" Fargo laughed. "Alfie's as big as a minute, Kitty. What can he do to quell disturbances?"

"He's hard as granite, Skye Fargo. You know that as well as I do. And he can handle a gun too. Near as well as I can."

All at once, Fargo realized that Alfie hadn't come out to say hello when he rode up to the cabin. He'd never seen Kitty without Alfie before, and a sick feeling attacked him. "Say, Kitty, where is Alfie?" He wasn't sure he wanted to know the answer.

She shrugged, hunched her shoulders, and started crying again. Fargo braced himself for the worst.

"I don't know where he is, Skye. I don't even know *how* he is." She buried her head in her hands and sobbed.

Fargo felt terrible. He'd always liked Alfie. "You think he might be dead?" he asked gently, afraid of sending Kitty more deeply into melancholy.

Kitty shook her head, not in denial, but to let him know she had no notion as to the state of Alfie's health. "I know they beat him up. He was laid up in bed for a long time, and I was tending to him, but I had to get out of town a week ago, and I haven't seen him since."

For some time, Fargo had been vaguely aware of a soft rattling sound, almost like the scrape of metal against metal, coming from somewhere inside the cabin. The howling wind almost rendered the scraping noise inaudible. He heard it again now. This time, it was followed by a loud groan. Then he heard the person in the other room cough twice and begin to cry feebly.

"Oh, Lord, I'd better go see if Sally needs more hot rocks in her bed. She's real bad off, Skye."

She sounded like it. Fargo rose and set his empty stew bowl on a rickety table. "Maybe there's something I can do to help."

Kitty gave him a look that told him how grateful she was for his words, and how little she believed either of them would be able to do anything for poor Sally Brown. Another miserable groan confirmed Kitty's prognosis for her friend's health.

They went to the other room. Fargo winced when Kitty pulled the blanket down to reveal the patient.

Fargo grunted involuntarily. He'd seen the results of beatings before. Hell, he'd administered enough of them and received his fair share. Until this minute, he'd not seen a woman so badly battered. He hurt, just looking at her poor swollen face.

"They busted her arm, Skye, and a couple of ribs. I think what's really bad, though, is that they kicked her. I think her spleen's busted."

Fargo shook his head, unable to think of anything to say. He had some laudanum in his pack. It wouldn't save Sally's life, but it might make the leaving of it less painful. "I'm sorry, Kitty. I wish there was something I could do, but the only thing I can offer is laudanum."

"That might help ease the pain some, anyhow. Other than that, I reckon the only thing we can do for her now is to try to make her comfortable. Any maybe pray."

They exchanged a glance. Fargo nodded. Sally's condition was hopeless, and he knew it as well as Kitty did.

Neither one of them was much on prayer; he knew that too.

He swore silently to himself and to Kitty and Sally Brown that he'd avenge the poor woman's death. Whoever Clay Franklin was, the bastard was going to pay for this.

2

Sally died no more than two or three hours after Fargo arrived at the cabin. He didn't know what time it was when her soul left the bonds of earth and pain. He only knew that the snow still fell and the wind still howled, seeping into the cabin through chinks in the old wood. He and Kitty had set about stuffing rags and crumpled paper into them, which helped a little. For the most part, however, they spent the time carrying heated stones to Sally's bed, taking away the cold ones, and reheating them by the fire.

They both took turns holding the dying woman's hand and talking softly to her. Every now and then, Sally would offer a weak squeeze, but Fargo didn't know if she understood what was happening. He felt mightily sorry for her. No woman should have to endure that.

He unearthed the flask of whiskey he had in his pack. He and Kitty tried to get some down Sally's throat, but she didn't seem to be able to swallow it. When the whiskey failed, they decided it was time for the laudanum.

"I don't want to give it to her too soon and have it wear off," Kitty told Fargo.

"I don't think we'd better wait any longer. I don't believe it'll have a chance to wear off. Better see if she can take some of it. It might help her when she . . . You know."

"Yes. I know."

Tears streaked Kitty's face as she carefully tipped the bottle to Sally's lips. Fargo massaged the sick woman's throat to promote a swallowing response, and in that way they managed to get the drug into her system. Sally seemed calmer afterward. Not long after that, she was gone.

Kitty wept softly in Fargo's arms. "Oh, Skye. She didn't deserve to have that happen. And it's all my fault."

"You said that before, Kitty. I didn't believe it then, and I don't believe it now. I can't imagine you wanting this to happen to your friend."

She pulled away and stared up at him, clearly outraged. "*Want* it to happen? Of course I didn't *want* it to happen!"

"Then I don't see why you say it's your fault." He wanted to ask her more about Alfie, but held off, knowing Kitty'd come to it in time. At the moment she was too rattled by her friend's death to talk about Alfie.

"I haven't told you the whole story yet." She sounded extraordinarily glum. "When I do, you might think it's all my fault too."

"I doubt it."

Kitty sniffled, plucked a handkerchief from her skirt pocket, and wiped her cheeks. Her eyes were puffy and red from all the crying she'd been doing. Fargo had never seen her in this state, and hated it.

"Listen, Kitty, why don't you collect yourself while I take Sally's body outside."

"Outside? You mean out into the storm?" Kitty's big blue eyes were dubious.

15

"It would be better. I don't think we ought to leave her in here."

He didn't want to go into details, but he'd been around corpses that had been left in heated rooms, and it didn't take long for them to start decomposing. While he had infinite respect for the Creator's plan for earth's creatures, he didn't necessarily want to smell His plan in action. Far better that Sally's body freeze outdoors than rot and stink in the next room.

Kitty, still sniffling, nodded. "Yeah, I suppose you're right. Oh, Lord." She started crying again.

Fargo was pleased to note that as much as she regretted her friend's passing, she was still as levelheaded as ever. He appreciated that quality in Kitty.

Sally didn't weigh more than a hundred pounds. Kitty had told him she'd been sick even before Franklin's men beat her up, and he imagined she'd lost weight during her illness. He felt doubly sorry for her when he realized how emaciated she'd been. The poor thing hadn't had any strength of body left to fight the results of the savage beating she'd been given. Fargo seethed at the thought of cowardly men who beat up on women.

He carried her through the still-falling snow and settled her as reverently as possible next to the barn. He figured she'd be frozen solid in an hour or two. He tried to think of a prayer to say over her body, but couldn't, so he only tipped his hat and left her there. He trusted God and Sally, if her essence still hovered around nearby, would understand that his intentions were good. The blizzard was so thick he damned near lost his way getting back to the door, and swore at himself for not tying a rope to the door handle.

He made it at last, and stumbled inside. Kitty knew better than to throw herself into his arms this time, but she did lead him to the fire, which she'd stoked until it roared almost as loudly as the wind outside. Fargo appreciated her thoughtfulness.

Holding his hands to the fire so they could thaw again, he decided it was time to hear Kitty's story. "All right. Tell me about this Clay Franklin fellow and why he thought it was such a good idea to beat a woman to death."

"He didn't only beat Sally up," Kitty said sadly. "He beat the stuffing out of a bunch of other people. Alfie, too."

Fargo eyed her, and her face crumpled up into tears again. "Oh, Skye! It was awful. Franklin came into Spanish Bend several months ago, and started buying up all the businesses in town. He'd make people low offers for their stores and such. At first, nobody would sell." She threw up her hands. "Why should they? He wasn't willing to give them anywhere near what the places were worth. Hell, most of the folks in Spanish Bend are just trying to make ends meet. They don't have anything to speculate with. They couldn't afford to sell low."

"Not many people can, no matter where they live."

She nodded. "I suppose that's so, but it's even harder here in the territory. I mean, we're all sort of pioneers here—doing everything on a shoestring."

She seemed to be getting herself worked up, so Fargo said soothingly, "I understand." He thought for a minute while Kitty took several deep, calming breaths. "Where'd Franklin come from?"

"Somewhere in Texas," Kitty replied.

That narrowed it down. "And he just rode into Spanish Bend and began buying it up?"

She nodded.

"Anybody know why? I mean, is Spanish Bend some

17

kind of important town?" He couldn't imagine it, but what did he know? The western territories were growing faster than he could keep up with.

"It's not too important yet, but it will be because folks are starting to raise cattle in these parts. The cowboys have to drive the herds north to the markets up there, because there's no railroad yet. Spanish Bend is halfway to Fort Sumner, and it acts as the hub for a lot of ranchers."

"A hub, is it?" Fargo's voice expressed his doubt.

"You know what I mean, Skye. It's as much of a hub as we got down here. All the ranchers need the place. It's where they come to get their supplies and so forth, and the cowboys spend the night when they're on the trail. When they get time off, they come to town because there's nowhere else around." She sighed heavily. "And when the Indians get restless and threaten folks in the outlying ranches and farms, they can come to town and hole up until their restlessness dies out."

"Or until the army makes the Indians die out."

"Yeah. That too."

It was Fargo's turn to sigh. He didn't go along with the wholesale slaughter of a native race, but nobody'd asked him before they started killing off the Indians. However, things relating to Spanish Bend were becoming clearer with Kitty's explanation. "So Franklin wanted to have himself a little monopoly out here in the middle of nowhere."

She nodded. "God knows, folks need a place like Spanish Bend. There isn't anything between here and Santa Fe and Albuquerque but a couple of forts, a bunch of Indians, and two hundred miles of nothing."

"I noticed that. Your letter reached me at Fort Sumner."

"I sent it in care of the army, because I knew they'd be

able to find you. I was afraid you might not get it for a year or more. I'm sure glad it didn't take that long, or I might be as dead as Sally."

She managed another quavery grin, and Fargo was proud of her. Despite all her hardships, Kitty was still full of spunk. "I can guess what happened next," he said. "When folks wouldn't sell, they'd have 'accidents.' "

"That's it, all right. Some of the so-called accidents were worse than others." She frowned into the fire, which made her features glow prettily. "It made me so mad, Skye. Franklin has a bunch of apes working for him, and they do all his dirty work for him. He pretends to be this hearty, laughing tycoon, but he's really a low-down, vicious murderer."

"I've met the type before."

"His men were mean to the women in town too. It wasn't only my girls."

Fargo lifted an eyebrow in inquiry.

Kitty shook her head sadly. "They raped more than one woman, Skye. Mrs. Gustavson died from the beating they gave her after they ravaged her. They got her daughter too. The poor kid's never been the same."

He saw Kitty's lips flatten out into a tight line. Fargo would have given a lot to have Clay Franklin and a couple of his hardcases within range of his Henry at the moment. "I'm sorry, Kitty. It must have been awful for everyone."

"Yeah, well, when he came to my place and offered me and Alfie half of what it was worth, I told him to stick his offer where the sun don't shine."

Fargo admired Kitty's resolution, but he was pretty sure Clay Franklin hadn't been of a like mind. "And I take it he didn't appreciate that."

Kitty's expression softened. "No. He didn't appreciate

it at all. He reminded me about how many accidents had been happening to folks in Spanish Bend who didn't sell out to him, but I was stubborn." She looked at Fargo through her eyelashes. "You know me, Skye."

"I sure do." He smiled at her to let her know he held her in high esteem, even if she was occasionally prey to reckless and ill-judged actions.

"So his thugs came in one night and tore up the place. Alfie tried to stop them and they near beat him to death. After what happened to Alfie, I couldn't find anyone who was willing to defy Franklin, so as much as I hated to do it, I gave up and started working for the bastard."

"When was that?"

She shrugged. "About two months ago. That's when I wrote to you, asking you to come here and help me out."

Skye eyed her narrowly. He knew that wasn't the end of the story; there was a dead woman outside to testify to it. "And then?"

Kitty heaved a gigantic sigh. "I should have waited for you, but I didn't. Alfie and Sally and me, we tried to take my saloon back, but we couldn't do it."

"I don't expect you could, unless you managed to drum up more than just the three of you."

"No. We figured on surprise, but surprise wasn't strong enough to overpower his army of brutes. Sally tried to rip into one of them with a broom, and that's when they beat her up." She stared mournfully into the fire and shuddered. "It was awful, Skye. It was just awful."

Fargo was silent for a moment, watching the firelight play over Kitty's features. "You probably should have taken his money and run for the hills."

"I know that now."

Fargo wished he'd kept his advice to himself when tears welled in her eyes and she started crying again.

"Hell, Kitty, you didn't want to give up your place. I understand that. It's not many women get to go into business for themselves. You ought to be proud you did it."

"You think so, do you?" She eyed him skeptically, her eyes glittering with tears.

"I do think so. And you'll get your business back too. I aim to see to it."

"Will you, Skye?"

"I will. Don't doubt it for a minute."

She looked so dismal that Fargo tried to think of something to cheer her up. Spying his empty stew bowl, he said, "Say, that stew was good, Kitty. I didn't know you could cook. I thought it was Alfie did all the cooking."

It worked. She took instant exception to his comment. All traces of sadness vanished, replaced by indignation. "*Alfie?* Skye Fargo, you don't know what you're talking about. Of course I can cook!"

"I reckon you can, if that stew is any example."

She tossed her head. "I've got lots of talents. Maybe you just don't recollect."

"I recollect some of them." He winked at her.

"Oh, Skye!"

And she was in his arms. He held her tight and rocked her back and forth.

"Make love to me, Skye. I feel so bad, and I know you can make me forget all this for a little while." She kissed him hard and rubbed herself against him.

"Are you sure, Kitty?" The notion sounded all right to him, but he'd never take advantage of a woman's unhappiness.

"I'm sure." As if to prove it, she ran her hand over the bulge in his britches.

He reacted immediately, tightening and growing under her practiced caresses.

"Please, Skye?" She smiled tremulously. "Here, let me give you some encouragement."

She stepped away from him and slowly unbuttoned the front of her gown, gazing at him the whole time with eyes that burned for him. He swallowed. He really didn't want to go to the bed in which Sally Brown had just died.

As if she understood, Kitty said, "We can use the bearskin rug, Skye. It'll be warm and cozy."

Her gown fell and puddled around her ankles. She stood before him in nothing but a corset and chemise, her breasts thrusting out against the thin material. Her nipples were hard already and teased his eyes. Then she slowly unhooked her corset, lowered the straps of her chemise, and she was naked as the day she was born, with only dark stockings and garters remaining—and they were certainly no barrier.

She was gorgeous. Her skin was as white as milk, her breasts large and firm. Her belly was barely rounded, her legs long and lovely, and Fargo itched to untie those garters and roll her stockings down while feasting at the tangle of dark blond curls beckoning to him at the juncture of her thighs. Fargo remembered burying himself between those silky thighs many times before, and his last restraint burst in a surge of lust. "You've convinced me, Kitty." He grinned. "Maybe you can help me undress now."

"I'd love to." She went to him, took his hand, and led him to the bearskin in front of the fire. He put his arms around her, and she started unbuttoning his shirt.

He groaned when she ran her hands through the hair on his chest. "You're quite a man, Skye Fargo."

"And you're quite a woman, Kitty O'Malley."

When she'd disposed of his shirt, flinging it aside as if

she were in a hurry, she knelt in front of him. Fargo's eyes drifted shut when she unfastened his belt, unbuttoned his trousers, and began to feast on the rigid pole her ministrations revealed.

He was about to explode, when she ceased torturing him, looked up, and smiled. "I feel better already, Skye."

"So do I," he managed to croak.

She patted the bearskin. "Why don't you come down here and join me, then."

He complied immediately, took her in his arms, and drew her close. He kissed her hard as his hands began a tactile survey of her luscious body. "You're as beautiful as ever, Kitty." He took one pebbled nipple into his mouth and licked greedily as his hand favored her other breast.

She sighed. "You know how to make a girl feel so good, Skye." She ran her hand over his bearded face. When he glanced up at her, she peered into his eyes. "You have the most beautiful blue eyes, Skye Fargo. I think it's a crime God wasted them on a fellow, when us girls need all the help we can get."

He laughed. "You look damn good to me, Kitty."

"Do I, Skye? Do I really?"

"You sure do."

"The last week or so has been pure hell. I figured it would show." She ran her fingers through her messy hair in a purely feminine gesture.

Fargo kissed her, and she sighed as she pressed her supple bosom into him. It wasn't long before they were taking full advantage of the bearskin, and the fire, and each other.

"It's been a long time, Skye honey," Kitty whispered in his ear as she ran her hand along one hard, hairy leg.

"Too long," he agreed.

Her hand ran up the other leg until it got to his crotch. She circled his stiff sex and gently ran her hand up and down. "Lordy, I've missed you, Skye! You know what to do to make a girl feel better."

She was making him feel a good deal better too. Life could get good at the strangest of times. This was a wonderful, life-affirming act after a lamentable, gloomy episode, and Fargo knew they both needed it.

"I think it's time to get rid of those garters, Kitty," he gasped after a minute, afraid he'd erupt before he'd taken care of Kitty.

"I think you're right."

He took his time, untying one garter then the other, then slowly rolling the right stocking down, revealing her beautiful thighs, then her calves, using his hands to tease her into a frenzy. After he'd tossed both black stockings aside, he knelt between her legs and used his tongue on her most sensitive bud. She was already wet and hot and ready for him, and she bucked under his ministrations. Fargo's manhood gave a throb in response.

Kitty said in a breathy rush, "Oh, Skye, that feels so good."

He was too preoccupied to answer, but he was pleased.

"I need you inside me, Skye," she said a moment later, sounding almost desperate.

"In a minute, Kitty. Don't be in a rush."

"A rush?" She offered a gasping laugh. "I'm about to explode, and I want you inside me when I do."

He could understand the reasoning behind her wishes, and agreed. "Glad to oblige." He left what he was doing, propped himself over her, and kissed her hard and deep, his tongue mating with hers in a frenzy of passion. With one deep thrust, he was fully inside her.

She gasped. "Lord, Skye, you feel so good!"

He withdrew as far as he could and plunged back in. "So do you." And he meant it sincerely. He drew out of her suddenly.

"Skye! Skye, what are you doing?"

"Taking my time." He grinned down at her, and leaned against her so that the tip of his manhood pressed against the nub of her pleasure. She sighed happily and arched against him.

Kitty's breasts were works of art. They were firm and perky and a perfect handful. And mouthful. While she rubbed herself against him, Fargo tongued one beautiful breast while he massaged the other. He took her hard nipple into his mouth and gently scraped his teeth against it. He suckled one, then the other.

"Lordy, Skye, you're driving me crazy."

Her skin was like silk, creamy and smooth and exactly what a man who'd been through hard times needed. Fargo judged Kitty had chosen the right profession—she was damned good at this.

"Skye, I can't stand it another second longer. You've got to be inside me right this minute!"

Fargo had about come to the same conclusion, so he pressed Kitty back and mounted her again, plunging into her dark, moist passage. He pumped in and out until Kitty dug her nails into his back, bucking like a wild horse, and he felt her inner muscles contract.

"Lord above!" she cried as she convulsed under him.

Fargo let go in a rush, pumping into her until he was drained. Sweat-drenched and exhausted, he collapsed on top of her.

They were both worn out when, several minutes later, he managed to ask, "Am I too heavy on you, Kitty?"

He felt her head shake beneath him. "I love the feel of you on top of me, Skye. You stay right where you are."

So he did. When he awoke a couple of hours later, they'd managed to work themselves into a cup-and-saucer arrangement that pleased him mightily since it placed her soft, warm buttocks right against his member, which had grown hard as he slept. Odd how things like that happened.

She turned into his arms and, with a deep sigh, began rubbing against him in her sleep. He smiled and massaged her silky buttocks. His stiff pole rubbed between her thighs, lubricated by moisture from her eagerness.

With a throaty groan, Kitty reached for his sex and guided him home. She was wet and ready, and so was he.

Their coupling the second time was slow and gentle. Kitty met each of his thrusts with an arch of her hips and a low moan. He felt her shudder a moment later, and he joined her in another fulfilling release.

3

The blizzard and its aftermath kept the Trailsman and Kitty O'Malley cabin-bound for three days. It wasn't until the fourth day that the snow had melted sufficiently to allow them to venture out-of-doors for essential errands. Skye chopped some more wood that day. There wasn't much left. What there was must have been hauled down from the mountains seventy-five or eighty miles to the southwest.

After he'd completed that chore, he checked on Sally Brown's body. He was glad to see that no animals had got to it. He wasn't sure Kitty was strong enough to handle any more grief at this point. She'd been through too much already, and was beginning to feel helpless, trapped in her cabin for so long.

They made good use of their time. When they weren't making love, they were plotting vengeance against Clay Franklin and his hirelings. Kitty had a lot of ideas that seemed a little gruesome to Fargo, but he figured it wouldn't hurt any to let her use her imagination to work out her hurt feelings. He'd take care of Franklin in his own way when he got to Spanish Bend.

On the fifth day, the ground was soft enough for Fargo to dig a grave to hold Sally Brown's body. Kitty tried to help, but she broke down, and he told her to go back inside the cabin and wait for him. But she refused, and instead began to brush Sally's hair and put some rouge on her cheeks and lips. Fargo didn't tell Kitty so, but he thought the paint made the poor thing look ghastly.

When the grave was deep enough, he laid Sally Brown solemnly in her final resting place, wishing he had a coffin. An old horse blanket he'd found in the barn had to suffice for a shroud. There was no spare wood for any kind of marker. After searching high and low, Kitty found some large rocks. She placed them on the grave to mark the spot and scratched Sally Brown's name on the biggest one.

Fargo knew how long that would last. A winter, maybe two with the endlessly blowing grit grinding away at those stones, and there would eventually be nothing left to mark the place where Sally Brown had been laid to rest. The knowledge gave him a frosty feeling in his soul that matched the wintry weather. He wondered if Sally had any family anywhere and, if she did, if they'd care that she was now gone for good. He debated asking Kitty, and ultimately decided not to. Kitty didn't need anything else to fret about.

Kitty murmured a prayer half remembered from her childhood. She got lost partway through, and subsided into tears of remorse.

Fargo shook off his own gloomy thoughts and put an arm around her shoulder. "We can't bring her back, Kitty, but we can at least get your saloon and the rest of Spanish Bend away from Franklin and his men."

She wiped her cheeks, sucked in a deep breath, and straightened her shoulders. "Yeah. Thanks, Skye. You're a real friend."

He grinned crookedly. "That's the best kind to have, I reckon."

She sniffled again. "I wish I had some flowers to put on her grave."

But it was winter, and it was the New Mexico Territory, and even in the height of summer, there weren't many flowers. Fargo hugged her hard and let her cry on his shoulder until he was sure she couldn't possibly have any tears left.

Shortly afterward, Skye Fargo saddled the Ovaro and resumed his interrupted trek to Spanish Bend. Before he left he made sure Kitty had plenty of food and wood to keep her fed and warm until he returned to report on his progress.

As if to prove its reputation for playing host to unpredictable weather, the New Mexico sun beamed down on him as he and the big pinto covered the few miles to Spanish Bend. The horse was frisky at first, restless from having been shut up and inactive for so many days. Fargo let him run out his fidgets. It felt good to canter along under the hard winter sunshine.

Patches of snow still lay on the ground here and there, but they were melting quickly. Around noon, Fargo estimated the air temperature to be around fifty-five or sixty degrees. He shook his head, marveling that as little as a week ago he'd damned near frozen to death in this same place. This territory kept a man on his toes with a vengeance.

When Fargo was a little more than a mile from his destination, he began to feel an uncanny prickling sensation at the back of his neck. He recognized the sign. He was under observation by somebody.

Without overtly appearing to do so, he scanned the landscape. He'd become accustomed to thinking of this part of the country as flat, but it wasn't really. There were sloping rises of land that passed for hills around here. A low, flat ridge of rock in the distance, sparkling with melting snow, ran alongside him for miles. Folks hereabouts called it Mescalero Ridge, which wasn't a comforting thought as the Mescalero Apaches hadn't taken kindly to white folks moving in on their territory. All things considered, Fargo would a far sight rather be stalked by Clay Franklin's men than a band of Apaches.

It wasn't long before his slight apprehension eased. The men watching him were white. No Indian would be so careless in his scrutiny of an unknown visitor as whoever his present observers were. Fargo could clearly see flashes of light as the sun glinted off of somebody's silver-bedecked hatband.

He didn't relax his guard, but he no longer worried much about his health. He doubted that even men as depraved as those Clay Franklin hired would shoot a lone rider out of his saddle for no reason.

Sure enough, before he'd gone another quarter of a mile, three men rode out from behind a rocky hillock and spread out in Fargo's path, obviously desiring to halt his progress. He pulled the Ovaro to a stop and showed his hands. No sense in riling them unless it proved necessary.

The three men rode abreast of each other. They appeared an unsavory lot to Fargo. The one in the middle, a big, ugly, pig-eyed, stubble-cheeked fellow with a huge sloppy gut hanging over his belt, had an air of pomposity about him. He was the one with the flashy hatband. Fargo figured him for the leader of this particular pack.

He nodded at the three horsemen. "Good morning, gentlemen. You from Spanish Bend?"

"That's for us to know," the fat man said smugly, as if

he thought he were being clever. Then he spat a wad of tobacco juice at the Ovaro's feet.

Fargo didn't so much as blink, but instead said in a mild tone, "I'm headed there, is why I asked."

"Headed there, are you?" said the one to the fat man's right, a skinny, sallow-faced man with mild, milky blue eyes. He followed his question up with a series of high-pitched "hee-hee-hee's." Fargo decided then and there that he might be a few cards shy of a deck.

The rider on the fat man's left scolded, "Shut up, Slim."

The man whom Fargo assumed was Slim stopped giggling, said, "All right, George," and shut up.

Fat Man said, "We sorta look out for keeping the order in Spanish Bend, stranger, and we come out here to greet you and to let you know that Clay Franklin don't tolerate anyone cutting up rough in his town."

His town? This was an interesting and rather sudden appropriation of other people's property, by Fargo's way of thinking. He nodded. "I don't cotton to trouble myself."

"No?" Fat Man jerked a nod at Fargo's Henry, residing in its saddle scabbard, then gazed pointedly for several seconds at his holstered Colt. "You're pretty well armed for a man who don't like trouble."

"A fellow's got to take care of himself when he travels alone, especially in the territory."

"That he does." Slim nodded, his head bobbing loosely on his skinny neck, his thick lips drawn into a grimace that was probably supposed to be a smile. "He shore does gotta take care of himself when he travels alone out here." He giggled again.

"I'm on my way from Fort Sumner," Fargo continued. "Headed to Spanish Bend to visit a friend."

"Yeah?" The fat man spat again. "Who's this friend, then?"

Fargo considered lying, but decided not to. "Fellow by the name of Alfie Doolittle."

Slim and George eyed each other around the fat man's paunch. George lifted a brow. Slim's mouth hung open.

Fat Man said, "Alfie Doolittle, huh? Where you know him from?"

"San Antonio. I used to gamble with him some there. I heard he was living in Spanish Bend. He still there?"

"Who wants to know?"

Fargo squinted at the fat man. He didn't like him a whole lot already, and they'd only just met. "Skye Fargo."

Slim let out a little squeak. George's eyebrow rose higher. Fat Man blinked twice. "Skye Fargo. No shit?"

"I heard of Skye Fargo," Slim said. "Damned if I ain't."

The fat man shifted in his saddle and frowned peevishly. "What business you got with Alfie Doolittle, Fargo?"

Fargo had decided while in the cabin with Kitty that he wasn't going to go out of his way to cause trouble in Spanish Bend. Not at first, anyway. He wanted to check out the lay of the land and see how best to solve Kitty's problem. He'd never, however, put up with lack of respect from other men, and he didn't see any reason to begin now.

He kneed the Ovaro and started him walking slowly toward the three men. "My business with Alfie is mine. I don't tell my business to folks I don't know."

"Oh, yeah?"

Fargo tensed, anticipating a reaction from his foe. He got one.

32

Fat Man's gun hadn't even cleared leather before Fargo's Colt was out and cocked and aiming at his gut, which made a very large target. Fargo saw him swallow. "I don't care to be drawn on for no reason either," he said in a soft, deadly voice. "What the hell's your name?"

"Shoot, George," said Slim, "Did you see that? I never even seen it! He was too fast for these old eyeballs. I heard about Skye Fargo. Damned if I ain't. And folks was right about him. Damned if they wasn't."

"Shut up, Slim."

"No need to get huffy, Fargo," Fat Man said. "Clay Franklin just hired me to watch out for trouble."

"I'm not trouble. I'm Skye Fargo."

"The one means the other, from what I've heard."

Fargo pulled the hammer back on his Colt.

Fat Man swallowed again. "You can put the gun away. I'm not going to do nothing. My name's Pearl. John Henry Pearl."

"Well, John Henry Pearl, unless Clay Franklin's got something shady going on that he wants to keep folks from seeing, it seems to me you're a little too quick to aim a gun at a man who's only riding to town to visit a friend."

"Shady? D'ya hear that, George? He asked if Franklin was shady." Slim giggled again.

"There's nothing shady going on," Pearl said. "Clay just wants to make sure no bad elements come to his town."

"Yeah? When'd it get to be his town?"

"When? Hell, Clay Franklin's a rich man. He bought it all up not long back."

"The townsfolk happy about that?"

33

Pearl shrugged. "They don't got nothing to bitch about. Franklin paid 'em all a fair price."

"I see." Fargo let the hammer down slowly when Pearl took his hand away from his gun butt with an exaggerated gesture, obviously wanting Fargo to think that he was acting in good faith. Fargo didn't believe it for a minute. His every nerve was snapping. He didn't admire these three or their tactics, and he certainly didn't trust them. He expected at least one of them to do something dirty.

He noticed the look on George's face a second before he heard the noise behind him, so he'd already kicked the Ovaro and turned in his saddle by the time a shot rang out.

With instincts honed from long, perilous years in the wilderness, Fargo no sooner saw his adversary—a stranger to him but not, he gathered, to his three foes—then he readjusted his aim. The man who'd shot at him screamed as Fargo's bullet tore through his hand. The gun flashed in the sunshine for a second before both gun and gunman went down, the man clutching his bleeding hand to his chest.

"Shit!" screamed Slim. "George, did you see that?"

George didn't even bother telling Slim to shut up this time. He was too busy drawing on Fargo.

He was too late. Fargo's bullet punched a hole in George's forehead, right between his eyes, and the man fell backward from his horse. John Henry Pearl, as slow as he was fat, stared at the commotion with his piggy eyes wide and his mouth gaping open. He didn't even try to draw, which showed either good sense, extreme sluggishness, or incredible caution. Fargo drew his own conclusion.

When the Ovaro quit dancing and Fargo knew the

danger was over, he aimed his gun at Pearl again "You want to try anything else, Pearl?"

"Hell, no! Jeeze, I didn't try nothing before." His nasal, whiny voice made Fargo wince. He hated whiners.

"It was that other guy what done it." Pearl gestured to the man weeping on the desert floor.

Fargo gestured with his gun at Slim, who drew his shoulders up, squinched his eyes, and grimaced, as if he expected to be shot any second. "Grab the bandanna from George's neck and tie it around that man's hand, Slim. First, though, give me your weapon. I don't fancy getting shot in the back when I start on my way to town."

Slim didn't so much as offer a yes or a no to Fargo's command. He just handed over his gun, slid from his mount, and walked to his fallen comrade. He stared at George's carcass for a moment before he knelt down and began undoing the knot at the dead man's neck. "Shoot, George. I'll miss drinkin' with you."

It was as good an epitaph as Fargo'd ever heard. "Hand me George's gun, Slim."

Slim did as he'd been asked.

"We can't give you our weapons!" Pearl sounded shocked. "Hell, what'll Franklin think?"

"I don't care what Franklin thinks. He ought to hire friendlier men if he wants them to hold on to their guns. Hand them over." Keeping Pearl covered, Fargo unlatched a saddlebag and drew out a canvas sack. He flapped it open. "Drop 'em in here," he said, holding out the sack.

"What're you gonna do with 'em?"

"I'll leave them with Alfie Doolittle." Fargo smiled at Pearl.

Pearl didn't like it, but he did as Fargo commanded.

His revolver made a clunking sound as it came to rest with the other men's hardware.

"Now the rifles, knives, and any derringers you happen to have hidden on you. Don't try anything funny."

With a furious frown, Pearl palmed a Colt two-shot derringer and dropped it in the sack, along with a razor-sharp Arkansas toothpick. "This ain't fair," he grumbled.

Fargo didn't bother answering. Slim looked sad as he went from George's body to the wounded man.

"Give me his gun," Fargo told him. "Don't try anything, Slim. I don't want to shoot you."

"I ain't gonna try nothing." Slim sounded too unhappy to lie. He might not have much brain, but he had more common sense than Pearl. Fargo watched as Slim dropped his friend's gun in the sack, then reached behind his back to fetch his knife. Fargo heard Slim sniff dolefully as he proceeded to bind his cohort's bloody hand.

"Pearl, why don't you tell me where I can find Alfie."

"He works in Franklin's saloon."

Franklin's saloon, was it? Well, Fargo guessed it was for the time being. He didn't argue. "Spanish Bend have more than one saloon?"

Pearl shook his head. "Too small."

"What's the place called?" Franklin inquired.

"Dammit, you'll see it, Fargo! It's right there, lookin' like a saloon." When the hammer on Fargo's Colt clicked back, Pearl licked his lips. He looked exactly like what he was: a bully who was only brave when he held all the cards. "It's called the Pecos Belle. Some female named it. You'll see it sure enough."

Fargo nodded and nudged his horse forward. "Better pick up your man there before he begins to rot." Fargo suspected that George had been rotten before he died, but he didn't share his opinion with Pearl, for Slim's sake.

Pearl grunted. "This ain't fair, Fargo. Anything can happen to a man out here on these plains who ain't got a weapon."

"You should have thought of that before you tangled with me, Pearl."

4

Spanish Bend looked like a dozen other southwestern villages Skye Fargo had visited: Small, ugly, windblown, and probably coated with as much dust inside as out.

Today the dust had been watered by melting snow into thick mud, and the Ovaro's hooves made a sucking sound as it moved through the muck. It looked as if very few of the town's buildings had been painted recently; most had never seen a coat of paint in their lives. Several of the wooden and adobe structures were pocked with bullet holes. Life in the territory had never been a peaceful affair.

Fargo had no trouble finding the Pecos Belle Saloon. It was as ugly, peeling, and windblown as any of the other buildings in town, but it was bigger, and it had a pretty painted sign hanging out front. Kitty had told him the painter accepted whiskey for his art. Fargo thought that was kind of pathetic, but he did admire the man's talent.

The Pecos Belle had two doors. The outer one, a thick wooden number, was meant to protect the drinkers inside from bad weather. It stood open today since it was moderately warm. The saloon's scarred inner batwing doors flapped constantly and seemed to disgorge and envelop small rivers of men, back and forth, in and out, as

Fargo rode the Ovaro down the street. From this phenomenon, he surmised that folks did a lot of drinking in the Pecos Belle. Either that, or Clay Franklin carried out his town-grabbing business from inside the saloon. Probably both.

At least ten horses were already tied up to the hitching rail outside the saloon. Fargo rode over to add the Ovaro to the row. Horses were gregarious creatures. He figured they'd be happy swapping lies, and flies, with each other while he made contact with Alfie Doolittle inside the saloon.

Alfie. This would be, perhaps, the trickiest part of this whole enterprise. If Alfie said anything to indicate that Fargo was a good friend of Kitty's, Clay Franklin would surely hear about it. If that happened, Fargo's job would become much harder, if not impossible.

It was also possible, although he considered it unlikely, that Alfie had turned his coat and was now in cahoots with Franklin. Fargo couldn't imagine Alfie turning on Kitty, but he reckoned stranger things had happened to him on the trail.

He dismounted and untied the sack of guns from where he'd attached it to the saddle. With the bag swung over his shoulder, he pushed through the batwing doors on the tail of two men who looked like ranchers, then stood aside with his back against the wall, and proceeded to survey the room. Fargo liked to know what he was getting into before he exposed himself to potential trouble.

One of the first people he saw through the dense fog of cigar smoke hovering in the room was Alfie Doolittle. He stood behind the bar and was at present pouring whiskey into a glass. Alfie appeared relaxed and happy, a state of affairs of which Skye wasn't sure he approved, although he'd be the first to admit a fellow had to make a living somehow. Whatever the actual state of Alfie's moral and mental processes, he was smiling and seemed to be chatting amiably with his customer. Skye's gaze left Alfie and traveled around the rest of the room.

The Pecos Belle was a nice place. Kitty had done herself proud. The walls had been freshly painted and hosted several paintings of scantily clad maidens. Sawdust had been sprinkled on the floor, and it looked as if it was swept out and changed frequently. The bar where Alfie worked wasn't a mere wooden plank set on ash barrels. It was made of dark mahogany, and it gleamed where Alfie wiped up a spill with his rag. Bottles were lined up behind it, and kegs of beer rested on a back shelf.

A polished mirror hung on the wall behind the bar, reflecting the folks drinking and playing cards at numerous tables in the room. The haze of tobacco smoke filling the air gave a gray-blue patina to the saloon and everything in it.

A couple of women in revealing costumes chatted with customers. The women didn't look awfully happy, but Fargo hadn't expected them to. A sporting girl's life wasn't a barrel of laughs. A flight of stairs led up to where Fargo assumed the girls entertained men. A long upstairs hallway with a wooden bannister overlooked the saloon. A series of doors, all closed at the moment, lined the wall.

As Fargo watched, one of the doors opened and a gent stepped out, looking sleepy and satisfied. Fargo expected that the girl who'd put the smirk on his face was still in the room, washing up, and would come downstairs to try to drum up more business as soon as she'd finished.

The Pecos Belle looked to be a thriving business. It

made Fargo sick when he considered how much work and money Kitty had put into it, only to have it appropriated by Clay Franklin through unscrupulous means. He turned his head when he heard a ruckus coming from a back corner of the room.

"But Mr. Franklin, if you'll only give me a little more time, I can come up with the money." One of the ranchers who'd entered the saloon ahead of Fargo was the speaker. He held one hand out in a beseeching gesture, his hat clutched tightly in the other hand.

A big man with a sleek, pink-cheeked face and an arrogant air about him sat with his back against the wall. His eyes, even from as far away as Fargo was, appeared cold and emotionless. Fargo pegged him as Clay Franklin immediately. He also expected the fellow who was pleading with him wouldn't get very far.

Franklin looked up at the rancher and smiled, his eyes as beady and unblinking as a lizard's. Two beefy men stood beside his chair. Enforcers, Fargo surmised, thugs hired to beat up on anybody who annoyed Clay Franklin.

"I've given you plenty of time already, Harry," Franklin said in a voice that dripped with threat. "I loaned you the money in good faith, and I've waited plenty long enough. I don't run a charity. You want charity, you'll have to go somewhere else."

"Yeah, go to a church. If you can find one." The thug at Franklin's right guffawed at his own wit.

The man who'd come in the saloon with Harry stepped forward. His face was red with anger on his friend's account. He hadn't removed his hat. "Dammit, Franklin, it's because of you that Harry needed the money in the first place. If your men hadn't torn up his fences and burned his barn, he'd—"

His words were cut off when Franklin made a quick

gesture, and one of the men flanking him grabbed the speaker. He gave Harry's friend a vicious punch to the stomach, and he doubled over with a grunt of pain.

Franklin motioned with his thumb. "You ought to tell your friend to mind his manners, Harry. And I'm not giving you any more time. You've had enough. If you value your health, I'd advise you to pack up your family and get off of that property before the end of the week. You never know what might happen to your wife and kids if you don't take my advice. As you know, there's been a terrible rash of accidents in and around Spanish Bend lately." He grinned evilly.

The other enforcer laughed. Harry lifted his hands again, then let them drop. Fargo had seldom seen such a helpless gesture.

"See Harry and his friend to the door, Barney," Franklin commanded one of his men.

The puncher roughly grabbed Harry's friend by the back of his jacket collar and pulled him up. "Let's go, you."

Harry turned away from Franklin, a forlorn expression on his face. His friend had managed to straighten up by this time, so his adversary released his jacket. He staggered a little bit, but managed to aim himself at the door. As the two men walked away from Franklin, Fargo heard him say softly, "I'm sorry, Harry."

"Hell, it ain't your fault, Abe."

Fargo hadn't been paying any attention to Alfie during this exchange. However, when the trio of men walked past the bar, he noticed that Alfie had taken to sweeping the floor. He also noticed that Alfie's broom somehow managed to get pushed right smack in front of Barney. The big enforcer clumsily fell to the floor with a loud thump and a curse.

The two ranchers scurried through the swinging doors before anything more permanent could happen to them.

"Oh, Jeeze, Barney, I'm sorry!" Alfie dropped the broom and rushed over to the fallen man.

Fargo grinned to himself. He ought to have known better than to have doubted Alfie Doolittle. Alfie might have to bend a rule to save his skinny hide every now and then, but he'd never desert a friend, much less Kitty, the woman whom he loved.

"Damn you, Alfie Doolittle. You did that on purpose!" Barney was scrambling to his feet. His chin was bleeding where he'd scraped it against the sawdust-covered floor, and his hands were bunched up into fists the size of hams.

"No sir, Barney. I never. I didn't do nothing on purpose. I was only sweepin' up, and I didn't know you was there, honest." Alfie began helping to slap the dust off Barney's clothes, and none too gently.

"Let him be, Barney." Clay Franklin evidently had enjoyed the show, because he was chuckling.

Fargo shook his head, amazed that anyone who cared so little for his men's health and dignity could hold on to employees for any length of time. He must pay them well.

Franklin continued. "It's only Alfie doing what Alfie does. You know he's thick."

Alfie? Thick? Fargo would have scratched his head in amazement at Franklin's assumption of mental deficiency on Alfie's part except that he didn't want to call needless attention to himself. Alfie had always been as sharp as a needle. As he studied his friend some more, Fargo noticed that Alfie did have a rather vacant expression on his wrinkled old face. Fargo wondered if the wily codger was putting on a show of stupidity for his audience. If he was, Fargo approved. Never show the enemy your cards was one of his favorite mottos.

"That's right, Mr. Franklin." Alfie tapped his head and gave Franklin a vapid, empty-headed smile. "I always was thick, right from when I was a baby. My ma told me so."

Fargo shook his head, amused by this display of dramatic talent on Alfie's part. Something suddenly occurred to him, and his amusement faded. He hoped to hell Franklin's badasses hadn't done permanent damage to Alfie's brain when they beat him up.

But no. Alfie was nobody's fool. Never had been, and wasn't now. It was a comforting thought, because Fargo now knew for certain that he'd have an ally as he worked to get Kitty's saloon back and avenged Sally Brown's death.

About a second after that notion crossed his mind, Alfie spotted Fargo for the first time. Fargo saw his eyes widen for no more than an instant before he went back to playing the blockhead for Clay Franklin's benefit. Since Barney was still glowering at him as he wiped his bloody chin, Alfie affected an air of sadness. "I'm sure sorry, Barney. I gotta be more careful where I sweep, I reckon. Ya need a wet rag or something?"

"Get the hell out of my sight, old man."

"Yes, sir. Yes, sir." Alfie scuttled behind the bar and propped the broom up in a corner.

A few moments later, the saloon returned to its usual business. The drone of men talking and playing cards, the clink of glasses, and the continuous swish of the doors resumed as if nothing had happened. Fargo walked over to the bar.

Alfie gave him a slanty-eyed glance that told Fargo it

44

was up to him to make the first move. Fargo appreciated Alfie's keen sense a lot right then.

"Good to see you, Alfie. How've you been?" Fargo held out a hand, which Alfie took and shook happily. He appeared relieved that he wouldn't have to act the stranger.

"God, Skye, it's been a long time. How you been?"

"All right, Alfie." Fargo gave him a big smile, lifted the sack he still carried, and set it on the bar. The weapons inside clanked. "You want to hold this for me? Some fellows will be in to fetch what's in it a little later."

A look of interest crossed Alfie's face. He took the sack, glanced inside, and whistled. When he lifted his head, Fargo could see the smile in his eyes.

"Where'd you get these here things, Skye?"

"Oh, I ran into a few men outside of town. I'm just holding those for them."

With a grin, Alfie retied the sack and shoved it underneath the bar. "It's good to see you, Skye. And unexpected. What you doin' in these parts?"

"Just riding through. Thought I'd stop by to see you."

Alfie nodded and grabbed for a bottle. "Bourbon?"

"Thanks." If he had any leftover doubts about Alfie's relative mental health, the offer of bourbon quelled them. Bourbon had always been Skye Fargo's drink of choice and if Alfie remembered that, he was still sound as a dollar. Probably sounder.

Alfie shot a glance around the saloon. Then, as he bent over the bar to pour Fargo's drink, he whispered, "You must have seen Kitty, Skye. Did you get her letter?"

"Yeah. Got it at Fort Sumner. I left her this morning. I helped her bury Sally."

Alfie's face screwed up in sorrow for a second and he uttered a soft, "Damn."

Fargo tipped the glass to his lips and drained it. Alfie refilled it immediately and whispered another question. "Who'd you take those weapons from?"

"Some of Franklin's men. John Henry Pearl, a fellow named Slim, somebody named George, and another man whose name I never caught. I met them on my way into town."

"And you disarmed them?" Alfie's eyebrows rose.

Fargo nodded and sipped bourbon. "George didn't make it."

Alfie shook his head. He looked slightly worried. "George, huh?"

"Yeah. He drew on me first."

"That don't surprise me none. George was a skunk."

"I noticed that about him. Slim seemed to like him."

"Hell, Slim likes everybody." Alfie chuckled briefly before he got serious again. "Well, all's I have to say is you'd better watch your back. Franklin don't like folks killin' his men."

"Didn't figure he would." Fargo leaned against the bar and scanned the crowd. Franklin, he noticed, looked at him, then quickly looked away. He beckoned to one of his henchmen and whispered something in his ear. The fellow squinted at Fargo through the tobacco smoke haze, shook his head, and said something to Franklin.

Alfie said softly, "They've pegged you, Skye. You'll have to watch yourself careful."

"Where can we meet, Alfie? We've got to talk."

"Get yourself a room at the Silver Dollar. Mr. Purvis runs the place, and he's a good man. Lost his hotel to Franklin and might be willing to help. Another bartender, fellow name of Jimmy, relieves me at midnight. I'll visit you at your room then."

Fargo grunted his assent.

Alfie said, more loudly for Franklin's benefit, "Hell, it's been dogs' years, Skye. What you been doin' with yourself?"

Fargo played along. "Not much, Alfie. This and that. Still contracting with the army every now and then when I need money. Otherwise, I'm a rambler. You know that."

"I do know it, Skye. I sure do." Alfie let out with a ridiculous laugh. If Fargo didn't know better, he'd honestly have believed the man was a half-wit.

Somebody bumped Fargo's shoulder, making him spill some of his drink. When he looked, he saw the second of the two henchmen who'd been standing with Franklin—the one without the bloody chin.

"Whoops," Alfie said idiotically. "He bumped ya, Skye."

"I noticed." Fargo eyed the man glacially. "He didn't apologize for it, either."

"Who the hell are you?" the man snarled.

Fargo sipped his bourbon. "Who's asking?"

"That there's—"

Fargo lifted a hand and Alfie quit babbling. "Let the man speak for himself, Alfie. He's got a voice, even if he doesn't have any manners."

"Listen here, you." The man made a threatening step toward Fargo, who lifted a hand and shoved him in the chest. The man staggered backward.

Fargo heard Alfie mutter, "Uh-oh." Instantly, the little man disappeared behind the bar.

"Why, you son of a—"

Before the man could get his weapon out of his holster, Fargo had drawn his Colt and aimed it at his gut. "I wouldn't if I were you, son. Now, what's your name?"

"To hell with my name!" The man was now furious, as well as humiliated.

With his back against the bar, Fargo had a clear view of the room. Not another soul in it stirred. Every eye in the place was directed at him and the irate would-be gunman whose arms were now held out to his sides as if he were just waiting for the Trailsman to blink so he could shoot him dead.

At that moment, the batwing doors swung open and Fargo's three friends from the desert walked in, looking tired, dusty, and ornery. The one with the bandaged hand held it gingerly. They stopped short when they took in Fargo leaning nonchalantly against the bar.

5

Slim said, "Well, hell, looky what's happenin' now, John Henry. That there's the Skye Fargo feller that done got the drop on Dewy."

After what seemed like a year to Fargo, during which the very air around him crackled with ill-suppressed violence, Clay Franklin spoke from his throne in the corner. "Where the hell have you three been? Where's George?"

Franklin glanced at the gunman still being held at bay by Fargo and appeared vexed. "Leave the man alone, Dewy. Hell, he was only havin' himself a drink." He sounded as vexed as he looked. Fargo didn't know if Franklin was annoyed with him, or with Dewy for his failure to kill him, or both. But he well knew that his health and well-being would depend upon always watching.

Dewy didn't want to leave the Trailsman alone. It was obvious in his bearing and the murderous glare in his eyes. What he wanted to do was kill Skye Fargo. Since, however, he apparently deemed it more prudent to comply with his boss than to try and shoot his enemy against Franklin's orders, he obeyed.

"George is outside slung over his horse," Slim said in answer to Franklin's question. "He's dead." He still stared, round-eyed, at Fargo, who hadn't put his Colt away.

49

"Dead?" Franklin frowned. "What the hell happened to him?"

"Him and Reggie both got shot by that there feller. He didn't kill Reggie, though. Just winged him. Fastest damn thing I ever seen. That there feller"—Slim pointed a skinny finger at Fargo—"he shot George right between the eyes. Pow! Just like that. I never seen nothing like it. We stopped him outside of town and he—"

"Shut up, Slim," said John Henry Pearl, who had been silent until now. He turned to Franklin. "This man's Skye Fargo, Mr. Franklin. He said he was headed to Spanish Bend to see Alfie. Claimed they was friends."

A ferocious scowl visited Franklin's face.

Slim started in again. "Well, George, he tried to shoot him, y'see, Mr. Franklin. And this here—"

"Shut up, Slim," Pearl said, then continued to speak to Franklin. "George tried to draw him down. Fargo was quicker." He hooked a thumb in the Trailsman's direction.

Tension continued to vibrate in the air. Franklin looked mad enough to spit tacks for several seconds. Then, after what seemed like a great deal of inner struggle, his aspect eased. He donned a congenial expression, but it didn't reach his eyes, which were still as cold and lifeless as Sally Brown's. Fargo wouldn't have trusted him farther than he could throw him.

"So George got a little hotheaded, did he? And Reggie too?" Franklin's lizard eyes glittered as he turned them on Fargo. "And this is the famous Trailsman? I've heard of you, Mr. Fargo, and about your skill with a gun."

There was a general whisper in the room. Skye holstered his Colt.

Alfie bobbed his head. "He shore is good with his, Mr. Franklin. Skye and me, we've known each other for a long damned time. We go back a long ways. Why, we knew each other—"

"Right," Fargo broke in quickly, not wanting Alfie to muck up the story he'd concocted for the benefit of Franklin and his men. "Met in San Antonio years ago."

Alfie didn't miss a beat. "San Antone. That's right. It was San Antone, waren't it, Skye?"

Franklin rose from his chair with a grunt. "Welcome to Spanish Bend, Mr. Fargo." He walked over to Skye and held out his hand. "Hope you enjoy your stay in our town."

Now it was "our" town. Fargo wasn't going to argue over terms. Not yet, anyway. Although he didn't much care to cozy up to villains, he shook Franklin's hand.

"I expect you've had quite a ride of it," Franklin continued, to all appearances the gracious host. "Did you meet anybody on your trip besides my overeager deputies here?"

The man was fishing for information, trying, Fargo was certain, to ascertain whether or not he had talked to Kitty O'Malley or Sally Brown. "No one but your ambassadors here." He shrugged at Slim, who stood there with his mouth hanging open, and Pearl, who looked like he wanted to join Dewy in beating Fargo to a bloody pulp, and Reggie, who continued to tenderly cradle his hand. Reggie looked more pained than mad, although Fargo wouldn't have offered money on the odds over which emotion prevailed in his breast.

Franklin spun around and glared at Slim, whose mouth clanked shut, at Pearl, who stopped scowling at Fargo, and at Reggie, whose demeanor soured. "Yes. They're a little too quick at jumping to conclusions about some things." He turned again to Slim, saying, "You say you brought George's body back?"

51

Slim swallowed and nodded.

"Then get on out of here and carry the body to the undertaker."

The two men left. Franklin eyed Reggie with loathing. "Get that hand washed and bandaged, Reggie. Doc Wilkins ought to be sober this time of day."

Reggie nodded once jerkily and left the saloon. Franklin then turned to Fargo. "We've got us some obliging ladies in the Pecos Belle, Mr. Fargo, if you're interested in a little companionship after your long trip." He winked at Skye. His friendly air still hadn't reached his eyes, which reminded Fargo of the leaden, slate gray sky outside.

"Thanks, Mr. Franklin. I think I'll just get a room and sleep for a while. Alfie told me there's a hotel called the Silver Dollar in Spanish Bend. He said that's the best place in town to stay."

"Right. That's my joint too." He looked smug. "Got nice rooms there."

Fargo tugged on his hat brim. "Thanks." He turned and tossed a coin to Alfie. "Good to see you again, Alfie. Maybe we can get together before I have to take off for Fort Stanton."

"Mebbe. Mebbe." Alfie's loose-jointed neck bobbed some more. "Good to see you, Skye. Good to see you."

Fargo took his horse to Gustavson's Livery Stable—which now belonged to Clay Franklin like everything else in town, he surmised—saw to the Ovaro's needs, and then walked across the street to the Silver Dollar Hotel. He didn't drop his guard for a second, but he made sure nobody watching him knew it. Although he saw no one, he was certain he was under surveillance.

He suspected that an attack, if it came, wouldn't be sprung on him out in the open. Franklin's kind didn't operate that way. Franklin would probably have his men sneak up on him when they thought he was sleeping. That way, Fargo's death could be chalked up to another unfortunate "accident."

There was nothing remarkable about the Silver Dollar. It wasn't fancy by anybody's standards, yet it was clean and respectable-looking. The man standing behind the counter seemed awfully gloomy. Fargo assumed he was the Mr. Purvis about whom Alfie had told him, which would account for his unhappy disposition.

He walked to the registration desk and smiled. "Are you Mr. Purvis?"

"That's right. Richard Purvis." He eyed Fargo warily, as if he didn't trust anyone who knew his name. Or anyone who didn't, for that matter.

"You've got a nice hotel here, Mr. Purvis." Fargo picked up the quill.

"Yeah," said the man. He looked even gloomier after he said it. "Thanks."

Fargo dipped the quill in the ink standard and, with it poised above the registration book, squinted at the man. "You don't sound real happy about your job."

The man shrugged and shifted his feet, uncomfortable about being questioned.

"How many other people do you have staying here right now?" Fargo asked the question casually.

"Nobody else at the moment. Spanish Bend isn't real popular as a holiday spot."

Fargo chuckled to let the man know he appreciated his attempt at humor. "Don't expect it is."

Purvis didn't smile back. Not a cheerful fellow, Mr. Richard Purvis.

With deliberation, Fargo wrote his name in the book, making sure he wrote it big enough for the other fellow to read it, even upside down. As Purvis eyed the name, his mouth fell open and his eyes went wide. "Skye Fargo. *The* Skye Fargo?"

"I don't know how many of us there are. That's my name, though."

"Hell." Purvis's mouth worked, as if he were struggling with himself about whether or not to spit out what was on the tip of his tongue.

Fargo decided to help him out. "I understand there's been some big changes in this little town recently."

Richard Purvis's bile finally bubbled over. "Changes? Changes? There's been hell to pay, is what there's been. I wish you'd come here six months ago. From what I've heard about you, you might have been able to stop it."

Fargo lifted an eyebrow in a gesture of inquiry. "Stop what exactly?"

Purvis now looked as if he wished he'd kept his mouth shut. After clearing his throat, he said, "Say, you aren't working for Mr. Clay Franklin, are you?"

"No. I'm an old friend of Alfie Doolittle's. I rode to Spanish Bend to see him since I was in the area."

"In the area?" The man's skepticism couldn't have been more apparent if he'd painted a question mark on his forehead.

Fargo grinned. "In a manner of speaking." Nothing was in the area of Spanish Bend, except hundreds of miles of barren prairie, a few Indian bands, some soldiers, and several small ranches that, Skye imagined, had the devil of a time making ends meet.

"Oh." Purvis fingered the quill now lying beside the registration book. "I'd kinda hoped you'd come here for something else."

"Oh? What might that be?"

Purvis cleared his throat again. "Nothing. Nothing." The man was definitely gloomy.

Fargo considered how to draw the hotel keeper out. He said carefully, "You sound like you don't much like the changes that have taken place in Spanish Bend in recent months, Mr. Purvis. I've heard lots of folks weren't happy about them."

The other man's mouth screwed up. Again it looked to Fargo as if he were battling between giving in to his urge to spew out his indignation or play it safe and hold his tongue. Indignation won. "Dammit, this used to be my place." He swung his arm in an arc, indicating the hotel. "It was a good business. It isn't the San Francisco Palace or nothing, but I made a tidy living serving the ranchers and cowboys and merchants and drummers that came through Spanish Bend."

"That so?"

"Yes. Until Clay Franklin swooped in like a damned vulture and took it over, like he took over everything else."

"How'd he do that?"

"Had those big hogs of his beat my son, Richie, until they damned near killed him, is how. I knew I couldn't fight him after that, because they wouldn't have stopped at just a beating the next time. Richie wanted me to hold out some more, but hell, I'm not a fighter, I'm an innkeeper!"

Fargo nodded. "I understand that sort of thing happened to a lot of folks in town."

"Pretty much everybody."

"Didn't anyone object?"

Purvis stared at Fargo incredulously. "Didn't we *object*? Of course we did! That's when Franklin's blasted 'accidents' started happening." His lips pinched up again. "I guess the worst hit was Miss Kitty, who owned the saloon. Franklin didn't touch Kitty. He ripped the hell out of her place, though. When that didn't work, he went after her girls and Alfie Doolittle." He shook his head. "The bastard." He aimed a wad of spittle at the cuspidor.

Fargo nodded. "Too bad."

Purvis glared at him. "Too bad? Is that all you have to say about it?"

"I reckon it is for now." Fargo went to the stairs. Right before he started to walk up them, he turned to face Richard Purvis again. "If it should happen that somebody decides to go to the trouble of taking your town back, I don't suppose you'd go running to Franklin and tell him about it, would you?"

The innkeeper's eyes went as round as billiard balls. "You mean it?" For the first time since he'd begun talking, a glimmer of hope sparkled in his voice.

"Just wondering, is all."

"Mr. Fargo, if you was to try to get our town back, there's not a man in town—except the ones hired by Franklin—who wouldn't do his damnedest to help you do it."

Fargo eyed the man for several moments. Then he nodded and continued up the stairs.

He went to the room he'd been assigned, unlocked the door, and heaved his saddlebags and an extra horse blanket onto a handsome dressing table.

Then he sat on the chair in front of the dressing table, laced his fingers behind his head, propped his feet on the bed, and waited for Alfie Doolittle to show up.

6

It wasn't much past midnight when the Trailsman heard the creak of floorboards and some barely audible footsteps out on the hall carpeting. He got up from his chair, silent as a wraith, and stood to one side of the door and waited. He didn't have to wait long.

Soon there was a soft knock. "Skye? Skye? You in there?" Fargo recognized Alfie's voice, even though it was pitched to a whisper.

Cautiously, Fargo turned the knob and pushed the door open without revealing himself. He'd learned a long time ago not to trust anybody too much and, while he trusted Alfie as much as he trusted any man, he didn't trust Clay Franklin an inch and wouldn't put any kind of dirty, sneaky trick past him—not even using Alfie as bait.

When Alfie's hand appeared on the door and his head peeked around to see where Fargo was, Fargo stepped out and grinned at him. Alfie blinked back.

"I'm alone, Skye."

"You sure nobody followed you?"

It was Alfie's turn to grin. "Yep. I think Franklin was going to have a couple of his men who was drinkin' in the saloon follow me. I seen 'em talking and looking closely at me, but it didn't work out. I'm alone."

"How do you know for sure?" Skye was curious because Alfie had such a devilish look on his face.

"I drugged their drinks. They're all sleepin' like babies. Franklin too."

Fargo laughed quietly. "Good for you. Will they know what you did?"

"Naw." He came inside as Fargo closed the door and turned the lock. "They think I'm stupid."

"After watching that act you've been putting on, I'm not surprised."

"Damned good actor, ain't I?"

Skye laughed. "You sure are."

Alfie crossed the room and sat himself down on a chair with a grunt.

He pulled a bottle and a couple of glasses from inside his coat. "Here. I brung some bourbon for you, Skye. I added it to Slim's account. Slim's so dumb, he won't ever even suspect." He poured a good snort of amber liquid into a glass and held it out to Fargo.

"Thanks." Fargo took the glass and sat on his bed, but aimed to wait until Alfie had drunk some of the bourbon out of his own glass before he tried it. He really did trust Alfie. It's only that he'd learned caution in a hard school and didn't aim to start getting careless now.

"Here's mud in your eye," said Alfie, and swallowed down a big gulp of bourbon.

After tipping his glass Alfie's way and saying, "Here's to you, Alfie," Fargo did likewise. He then looked Alfie over critically. "Kitty told me they beat you damned near to death. You look all right to me."

"Shoot." Alfie took another drink from his glass and shook his head. "I look all right now. But for a couple of weeks there, you couldn't tell my face from a pumpkin, except pumpkins ain't purple. That was three months ago, though, and thanks to Kitty I pulled through all right. The cold weather still plays hob with my leg where they kicked me, though."

"I'm sorry you had to go through that, Alfie." Skye meant it sincerely.

"Yeah. Me too. I'll be all right, though. Hell, I'm gettin' old anyway. I been feelin' aches and pains for a couple of years now."

"You'll never get old, Alfie."

"So you say." Alfie chuckled and drained his glass. As he poured himself another one, he took a deep breath. "You say Sally wasn't as fortunate as me?"

Fargo drank and shook his head. "We buried her at a cabin a few miles off."

Alfie stared at the floor for a moment before he lifted his head and sighed. He looked sadder than Fargo had seen him in all the time they'd known each other. "Yeah. I know the place. Kitty said she was takin' her there. I give her some food and blankets and such-like. Didn't have no kind of medicine, although I tried my damnedest to bandage the poor woman up before they took off. I'd hoped it'd be enough."

"It was for Kitty. Sally was too far gone already, I expect. Kitty said Sally'd been sick even before Franklin's men got to her. She didn't have the strength to survive the beating too."

"Yeah." Alfie sounded glum. "Them bastards wouldn't leave her be, either. Kitty told 'em they could have any of the other girls they wanted, even her, but that Sally was sick and needed to rest. Clay, he always favored Sally, though, and kept workin' her. I understand he wasn't gentle about it."

Fargo chalked up another point against Franklin. Any man who'd take a woman against her will or while she was sick and needed rest was lower than dirt. "He favored the woman, so he used her when she was sick and then had his men beat the crap out of her?" Fargo asked incredulously.

Alfie shrugged. "He got mad when she said she didn't want to—you know."

"Yeah. I know."

"So he slapped her around a little to make her behave. That's what he said, anyway, to make her behave."

Fargo frowned, bile rising in his throat.

"And then, when his men got to beating on me—this was the second time, you understand, when Kitty and me was trying to get the saloon back—she tried to fight 'em off with a broom. That's when Franklin had them go after her. Well, you know how bad they beat her."

"Yeah. I saw her."

"Anybody'd do that to a woman is worse than scum." Alfie stared at him with eyes so glum, they reminded Skye of those of an old, worn-out hound dog.

He shook his head sympathetically. "I'm sorry you've had such a hard time here, Alfie."

"It ain't me so much as Kitty and Sally. I couldn't talk the doctor into seeing Sally, either. He's as afraid of Franklin as everybody else in town."

"Clay Franklin is a real prize, isn't he?"

"That he is." Alfie drank down some more bourbon and looked grim. "So how's Kitty, Skye? Her and me, we're like kin, you know."

"I know. She'll be fine. She was pretty torn up about Sally."

"That's Kitty, all right. She really cares about her girls." Alfie fiddled with his glass, turning it around in his hands before lifting it to his lips and draining it with a big gulp. When he looked up at Fargo, his eyes were watering; Fargo didn't know if it was from emotion or the liquor. "The truth is, Skye, Kitty and me—well, we might really *be* kin. I like to think we are."

Surprised, Fargo tilted his head and stared at him. "Kitty never told me anything about you being related."

"She don't know anything about it. And I don't ever aim to tell her."

Eyeing him curiously, Fargo said, "You want to explain that one to me, Alfie?"

Alfie's mouth worked a couple of times, and he seemed to be searching for the right words. All at once, as if he had to hurry before he lost his nerve, he burst out with it. "I might be her pa." He held up a hand to forestall any shocked outbursts from Fargo. "I know, I know. What kind of pa would let his little girl do what Kitty does, huh?"

"I didn't say a word."

"But the thing is, Skye, I might not be, too. But even if I'm not, I like to think of her as my little girl. See, she and me, we met in San Antone and we got to talkin' one night. I liked her from the first, because she's smart and funny and—well, hang it, she's a nice woman. Ain't her fault she had to do what she had to do."

Fargo nodded again. He knew that as well as anyone. Most folks, when push comes to shove, will do what it takes to survive. If pleasuring men is what Kitty had to do to survive, he wasn't about to cast stones—especially since he appreciated sporting girls a lot himself.

"Besides, she reminded me of someone."

Noting the faraway, melancholy expression on Alfie's face, Fargo decided to remain quiet. He figured if Alfie wanted to tell him more, he would. After heaving an enormous sigh, he did.

"Anyhow, when we got to talkin', she told me about herself—you know, about when she was a little girl growin' up and such. Her ma was dead, and she said she never knew who her pa was, but she was from Galveston. Well, Skye, twenty-some years ago when I lived in Galveston, a pretty girl and me, we was like this." He held up two fingers pressed together. "I went and joined the army to beat the Mexicans out of Texas, and—well . . ." His words trailed off.

Fargo nodded. He knew how it had been. As much as Alfie had loved his girl, like many men after the war, he hadn't quite gotten around to going back to San Antonio after her when Texas became an independent republic. At least not right away.

"I did go back for her," Alfie continued, answering Fargo's unasked question. "But I couldn't find her anywhere. Her family had left, and nobody knew where she'd gone to. Kitty told me that her own mother's ma and pa turned her out of the house when they found out she was going to have a baby. It might have been my Mary Belle, and the baby might have been mine." Along with sadness, intense guilt wracked Alfie's face. He seemed to shrivel in his chair under its influence.

"Anyway, that's who Kitty reminded me of. Mary Belle. And I decided that even if I'm not her pa, mebbe I can make up a little for what I done wrong by acting like a pa to Kitty." Alfie stared into his empty bourbon glass, as if he could find some explanations there. Fargo knew better. So did Alfie.

Fargo waited a couple of seconds and said, "I'm sorry, Alfie. It must have been hard on you to think about your Mary Belle having such a hard time of it."

"It was a hell of a lot worse for Mary Belle, living through it." He stared at the floor between his boots for a moment. "Damn, I loved her, Skye. And I treated her real bad."

Fargo didn't deny it. No matter how much Alfie regretted having left her, regrets paid no tolls. He didn't have to add to Alfie's grief by saying it, so he kept still.

It was as well he did, because he heard an almost imperceptible noise from outside in the hallway during those few silent seconds. He was on the alert instantly.

Alfie heard it too, and lifted his head. He opened his mouth, but Fargo raised a hand to stop him from speaking. Getting up from the bed, he made his way across the floor, sliding a braided rug along with him so his boots wouldn't clunk on the floorboards.

Someone was jimmying the lock. Fargo gave a signal to Alfie to sit still, and he stood beside the door, ready to take care of any intruders should they enter the room. He was so keyed up to attack, in fact, that he nearly broke the girl's neck when she shoved the door open and walked into the room.

Alfie shot out of his chair as if he'd been goosed. "Violet!"

"Hey, Alfie. How you doin'? I hope you don't mind that I—"

Her greeting ended in a screech when Fargo grabbed her and flung her to the floor. He was only just in time, because the man who'd followed the girl fired right before Fargo's Colt came down on his head. He heard the crack of metal against bone, and the villain's cry of rage and pain was cut short as he slumped to the ground.

Alfie sat with a thump. Holding his glass, his eyes as round as pie platters, he muttered, "Damn."

"Guess not all of them were asleep." Fargo wasn't even out of breath, although his nerves twanged. His glance fell to the girl on the floor, who was staring, horrified, at the unconscious man littering the doorway.

"My land," she whispered. "Joey."

Holding a hand out to help her up, Fargo said, "Sorry I had to be so rough on you, ma'am. I guess you didn't know he'd followed you?" Personally, he was withholding judgment. From the looks of her, she hadn't been in cahoots with the man on the ground, but he couldn't know for sure.

"No. I had no idea." She frowned. "Joey's kinda sweet on me. Maybe he followed me because he was jealous."

Violet took Fargo's hand as he helped her to her feet with some difficulty. From the rapidity of the pulse in the wrist which Fargo held, she'd been genuinely rattled. Whether that was from the shock of seeing a man attacked right in front of her, or from seeing the wrong man go down in the fight, Fargo didn't know.

He looked at Alfie. "You know this man?" He gestured at the body.

"One of Franklin's men. Joey Scarlet. Violet's probably right about why he followed her. He's raised hell more than once about her and other men."

The girl nodded as her eyes filled with tears. "Oh, my God." She teetered to the bed and collapsed on it, putting her face in her hands.

"Here, Violet," Alfie said kindly. "Take a swig of this. It'll calm you down some."

"Thanks." Violet took the glass from Alfie and drank its contents, choking and coughing at the burn in her gullet.

Fargo inspected her keenly. She couldn't be more than sixteen or seventeen years old. Not that being so young was unusual for a sporting girl. Hell, half the girls who came out West were orphans from back East seeking a better life for themselves, just as the men were. The women had fewer choices, however, and often ended up in Violet's profession out of desperation, if not by choice.

He gestured to the body on the floor. "Want to help me get rid of this, Alfie?"

Alfie was up in an instant. "Sure thing, Skye. What we gonna do with him?"

"I'll think of something. Let's take him down the hall first. I don't want to have him lying around in the way all night."

Fargo and Alfie each grabbed Joey Scarlet's arms and legs and carried him down the hall.

"We might as well let him wake up here as anywhere," Fargo said as he eased Scarlet's torso into a reclining position against the hall wall.

"When he comes to, he might report to Franklin," Alfie said with a grunt as he too set down his burden.

"Maybe. But if Violet's right about him only being jealous, it won't matter. Franklin probably won't care."

"Yeah. You're probably right." Alfie dusted his hands together.

Neither he nor Alfie said a word as they walked back to his room. He didn't know what to expect when they reentered, but Violet was there, still sitting on the bed, still holding the empty glass, looking dejected. She lifted her head when the door opened and watched them cautiously.

"Sorry we had to meet this way, Violet." Fargo kept his voice businesslike because he wasn't yet sure of the girl's intentions. "Did you come here to see me?"

She bobbed her head and squared her slender shoulders. "Yes. I followed Alfie. I figured you and him was going to talk about getting the saloon away from Franklin and giving it back to Miss Kitty, and I aim to help you."

"You do, do you?" He wasn't sure whether to be amused or offended.

She nodded, and he noticed she had a firm, determined little chin. He decided he was amused. "I'll have to think about that, Violet."

"Don't think too long, because I'm *going* to help you."

The girl was feisty. Her eyes were big and brown and soft as a fawn's, and he felt a pang of compassion for her. He didn't let it linger. In his line of work—and in hers—there wasn't room for compassion. Since there was only one chair in the room, and since he didn't particularly want to sit next to her on the bed, he walked over to the night table and picked up his empty glass. Turning back, he began to question her.

"You didn't know this Joey Scarlet character was following you here? You didn't hear him?"

She shook her head. "God, no. I'd never have come if I'd known. I reckon the wind was blowing too hard to hear anything. As jealous as he is, he might have killed you." She put the glass down with a clunk and hugged her shawl tight around her shoulders. "Or me."

Fargo nodded, but said nothing. He held his glass out for a refill and Alfie poured more bourbon into it. He judged that his silence would make the girl nervous, and he was right.

She fiddled with the fringes of her shawl and then blurted out, "Kitty used to talk about you a lot, Mr. Fargo. I—I was hoping I could persuade you to help us get her back to running the Pecos Belle. She's the only one's ever been nice to me since I started the sporting life." She dropped her shawl, clutched her hands in her lap, and stared at him and Alfie, plainly ashamed of herself and the business she was in.

Again Skye felt a lick of compassion which he squelched. "How can I know that, Violet? Begging your pardon, but if you were to take any information I might divulge back to Clay Franklin—"

"I'd never!" A flush of crimson invaded her cheeks, and she looked mad enough to thrash him—or at least try to thrash him—for a second or two.

Fargo's mouth lifted in a grin. He turned to Alfie. "Alfie? What do you think?"

Alfie considered the girl on the bed for a minute. "Violet here, she's a good girl, Skye. She's too blamed young to be in the business she's in. Kitty knew it and tried to take care of her, but she's a stubborn girl."

"Yes," Violet agreed. "She did. Kitty's the only one who's ever been nice to me in my whole life." She sniffled miserably. "It was a dirty shame, what Franklin and his men done to her and to Sally. It was a real crime."

"It was a crime, all right. They killed Sally."

The girl gasped, horrified.

"Too bad there's no law around here to take care of them for it."

"Ain't that the truth," said Alfie, his tone grim. "The sheriff was the first one Franklin got rid of. Then he put one of his men in his place."

"Exactly." Violet nodded vigorously.

"He's a bastard too." Alfie spat, his mouth twisted into a horrible grimace.

"They're all bastards." Violet sounded very definite in her assessment.

"I'm not surprised to hear it." The more Fargo heard about Franklin and his crew, the more he wanted to clear the men out of town.

Violet's visage brightened, and when she looked up at Skye, her big brown eyes were wide with hope. "So will you help us? I mean, can I help you? Lord, Mr. Fargo, somebody's got to help, or Mr. Franklin will kill us all. He's an animal. He's cruel with the girls. He likes it real rough. They all do."

She blushed, and despite her profession, Fargo was charmed by her beguiling innocence. "I think you ought to go on back to the saloon for now, Miss Violet, and let Alfie and me talk for a while. If we decide to do anything and you can help us, Alfie will let you in on it." He smiled at her, hoping her feelings wouldn't be hurt. "All right?"

The hope in her eyes died. Skye was sorry to see it go. "You mean you don't want me to stay? I got no money, Mr. Fargo, but I'm willing to pay however I can."

Her cheeks flushed red again, and Fargo knew exactly how she aimed to pay him for helping the girls at Kitty's saloon. He felt sorry for her. "You don't have to pay me, Violet. Alfie and Kitty are old friends of mine. I'll do a lot for friendship that I wouldn't do for money. Maybe, when this is all over, you can thank me then."

Her head drooped and she sniffled again. "You don't want me, huh?"

Fargo sat on the bed next to her and put an arm around her. "That's not it, honey. Honest. But Alfie and me, we've got a lot of things to talk about before we decide what's best to do."

"Skye's the most honest man I know, Violet. He's tellin' ya the truth."

Fargo had never been keen on bedding adolescents, although he might make an exception for Violet after this business was solved. She was a sweetheart, she had a lot of spirit, and she was offering the only thing she had to give. He was touched. He squeezed her shoulder gently. "All right, Violet? And don't say anything to the other girls until Alfie says you can. Will you do that?"

"But I want to help."

"The biggest help you can be to us right now is to keep quiet about coming to see Alfie and me tonight."

Her faun brown eyes peered into his lake blue ones, and she nodded unhappily. Skye thought that if the world were a just and equitable place, little Violet wouldn't be offering her body in payment to a stranger for a job that shouldn't need doing. She'd belong to a family that would take care of her and give her hot cocoa and cinnamon buns when she got upset, as she was now.

But this wasn't a just and equitable world. It was the New Mexico Territory, and a girl had to be as tough as tanned buffalo hide to survive in it. He knew Kitty was. And he hoped Violet was too.

"Be careful goin' home, dearie," Alfie said. "You want me to walk you back?"

"No thanks, Alfie. I'll be all right." She cocked her head to one side and looked puzzled. "All the men were sleeping when I left. I never saw anything like it. The place sounded like a lumber mill with all the snoring going on."

Fargo and Alfie glanced at each other. "How strange," said Fargo.

"Real strange," said Alfie, and he gave Fargo a sly wink.

Violet pulled her shawl around her shoulders. Skye would have preferred to see her back safely, but he couldn't do much about it now. The saloon was only a few steps away from the hotel, anyway.

Nevertheless, he had an uneasy feeling in his gut when Violet left his room. He watched her until she got to the stairs, then he returned to his room and peered down at her from his window. The light was so poor—only a few low-burning kerosene lamps hanging from hooks outside a building here and there—that he could barely make out her form as she hurried through the freezing night to the shelter of the saloon. He didn't see anyone following her.

"That's no way for a kid her age to make a living."

Alfie sighed. "She's not the youngest by far, but she does all right, I reckon. At least she did, until Franklin came to town. At least she ain't taken to drink nor to laudanum like some of 'em do to keep from feelin' things."

Fargo's determination to rid Spanish Bend of its usurping tyrant redoubled.

He and Alfie talked for an hour or more after Violet left them. They decided the best thing Alfie could do was watch and listen and keep Fargo informed of any plots or sinister plans Franklin and his men might hatch. He might drop the occasional dollop of laudanum into a glass of rye if it seemed prudent to do so in order to protect one of the girls, but Fargo told him not to overdo it, or Franklin might get suspicious. Other than that, Skye wanted Alfie to stay well out of the action until he needed him. He knew what to do. He'd done it before.

"Thanks, Skye." Alfie walked to the door and offered Fargo his gnarled hand.

Fargo shook it gladly. "Don't thank me yet, Alfie. I haven't done anything."

"You will," said Alfie with conviction.

Fargo appreciated his confidence.

"And I'll prime the girls, so they'll know to keep mum when you show up at the saloon."

"Thanks."

After Alfie left, Fargo carefully stuffed his blanket and a pillow under the covers of his bed to make it appear as if there was a man sleeping in it. He scattered a few personal articles around the room so that nobody who happened to enter would suspect the lump in the bed wasn't his own revered carcass.

Then he went to the room next to his, tried his key on that door, and discovered to his satisfaction that it worked just fine. He entered and locked the door behind him. He removed his boots and gunbelt, stowed his Henry rifle within easy reach, and coiled his gunbelt on the night table, with the butt end of the Colt forward for a quick grab. Then he made a thorough survey of the room, including the windows and their relationship to the street below, before he lay down to take a nap.

He hoped he'd get at least a couple of hours of rest before Franklin's men showed up to shoot at the pillows next door.

7

Skye Fargo had been sleeping peacefully for four hours before the silence of the night was shattered by gunfire in the room next to the one in which he slumbered. Because he'd had lots of practice at this sort of thing, he awoke instantly and rolled off the bed, grabbing his Henry as he went. He was already on his feet and alert as he picked up his Colt as well and hurried, stooping, across the room to the door.

He wasn't surprised by the violence. He'd already come to the conclusion that Joey Scarlet hadn't been sent by Franklin to do him in. Violet was undoubtedly right about Joey, who had probably only followed her because he thought she was going to another man's room. Whatever Joey Scarlet's mission had been, Fargo imagined the party next door at the moment was the officially designated group of assassins Franklin had sent to kill him.

Standing to one side, he pushed the door open a crack and peered out. One of Franklin's men had been assigned to stand guard outside the room next door, but he seemed unmistakably unfit for his job. Instead of watching the hall, the fool was staring at the door, as if he wished he could see through it and observe what he presumed was the bloody battle being waged within.

Fargo, bootless and in his stocking feet, crept up behind the guard silently and cracked him on the back of his head with the stock of his Henry. The man folded up like a concertina. Fargo caught him before he could make a telltale thump that might be heard by his comrades, and settled him gently on the floor to one side of the door. Then he waited.

Noises came from inside the room.

"Goddammit, put that down, Slim."

"But, John Henry, can't I just take a look?"

"No," another voice said—Fargo thought he recognized it as belonging to the man named Dewy. "Mr. Franklin said we aren't supposed to touch anything. Just do the job and get out, is what he said. You heard him yourself, Slim."

"Well, hell, I'd like to see Skye Fargo's guns up close." Slim sounded sorely disappointed. "It ain't like you get to see the guns of a man like him every day."

"Shut up, Slim," advised John Henry Pearl.

Fargo heard the rustle of bedclothes and braced himself.

"Shit!"

"Why, John Henry Pearl, it ain't nothin' but pillers! And look at them feathers a-flyin'."

"Shut up, Slim."

Slim sneezed.

"Let's get the hell out of here. Wherever he is, he must have heard the noise and figured out what's going on by this time."

The first man through the door was John Henry Pearl, who spotted Fargo and lifted his gun to fire. Fargo's Colt blasted him back inside the room less than a second later. His lifeless body careened into Slim, who screamed.

Dewy showed up next, blinking with befuddlement.

73

As soon as he spotted Fargo, he threw his gun down and lifted his arms. "Don't shoot. I'm unarmed."

"The pillows in that bed were unarmed too," Fargo told him, his voice as crisp as winter's frost.

He heard a frantic scrambling from inside the room and then heard the window being shoved open. He called out, "Don't try it, Slim. The drop would kill you, and if it doesn't, I sure will. You'd make a perfect target from that window, especially with both of your legs broken."

He heard a sob from the direction of the window. Two or three seconds later, Slim appeared, tears pouring in muddy streaks down his cheeks, his trembling hands in the air. Dewy looked disgusted.

"You probably should go into another line of work, Slim," Fargo said, not unkindly. "This one doesn't seem to be quite right for you."

"That's the truth, Mr. Fargo. That's the damn truth." Slim's voice was thick with misery.

The pounding of footsteps on the stairs sounded, and Fargo saw the hotel keeper, tying the belt to a plaid robe over his stomach and panting furiously, emerge from the stairway. He was balancing a lantern in one hand with difficulty as he fumbled with his robe. He blinked at the three men in the hallway, then at the still-unconscious man at Fargo's feet. "What's going on up here? What was that terrible noise?"

"Just a little accident, Mr. Purvis. Why don't you go on back to sleep now." Fargo smiled at the hotel keeper and gestured to Slim and Dewy. "Some folks came to pay a call on me."

Purvis eyed the man out cold on the hall floor uncertainly, and peered at the Trailsman. For a second, it looked as if he wanted to ask about the Colt Fargo had trained on Slim and Dewy. He evidently thought better of asking anything at all because, still looking confused, he backed toward the stairs. "All right, I'll go. But please try not to make a mess."

"We'll try. I'm afraid you might have to do some mopping-up in that room, though." Fargo gestured with his gun toward the open door. John Henry Pearl's left foot, its booted toes pointing toward the ceiling, poked out of the doorway. Fargo was grateful Purvis couldn't see the puddle of blood that had spilled onto one of the braided rugs.

Purvis opened his mouth, shut it again, and retreated with his lantern. Fargo presumed he didn't aim to get involved until he had to.

Dewy demanded, "What are you going to do now, Fargo? Shoot us? Give Purvis something more to clean up?"

Slim whimpered and wiped the back of his hand across his tearstained cheeks.

"No, I don't think so. I think I'm going to take the two of you to Mr. Franklin and ask him why four of his men came up here tonight to kill me." He smiled thinly at Slim and Dewy.

Slim gawked back at him, his slack mouth gaping, his mind, if he had one, a blank. The look of disgust on Dewy's face vanished and was replaced by an expression of consternation.

Fargo tilted his head to one side. "What's the matter, Dewy? Don't you like that idea?"

Fargo understood why Dewy appeared so unhappy. Dewy knew his boss well enough to be certain that Franklin would deny sending these men to assassinate Fargo in his bed. He'd probably have them hanged for attempted murder when the sun came up, thus preventing his own part in the scheme from coming to light. As if everyone wouldn't already know Franklin himself was behind it.

Dewy stammered, "Uh . . ." and Slim's mouth flapped a couple of times, but no words emerged from either of the two.

"Tell you what," Fargo continued. "If you fellows will give me your word that you'll get on your horses and head out of town—and not come back—I won't kill you, and I won't hand you over to Franklin either. What do you say to that?"

Slim's Adam's apple bobbed as he swallowed. He glanced at Dewy, obviously praying for inspiration from that direction, since his own brain was too feeble to take in and deal with such a momentous offer on its own.

Dewy said, "How the hell can we trust you?"

Fargo shrugged and smiled again. "I don't rightly know that you can."

The answer didn't please Dewy, but he didn't fuss about it. "How'll you be able to trust *us*?" He sounded skeptical.

"I don't expect I can trust you, Dewy. But if I see either one of you in Spanish Bend again, I'll shoot you, no questions asked. I don't deal in second chances. How's that for a bargain? You can take your friend here with you." He rested his sock-encased foot on the man in the hallway.

Slim swallowed again audibly and remained silent.

Dewy jerked his head toward the body littering Fargo's room. "How you going to explain that?"

"That's not your business, Dewy, although I certainly do appreciate your concern.

"Yeah." Dewy spat on the floor. "Sure you do. What about our weapons?"

Fargo shook his head. "Sorry, boys. I'm giving you a chance, but not that much of one. I'll take your guns."

Slim's eyes opened wide. "Does he mean he's gonna let us loose on them plains with no guns, Dewy? But—but, what about them Indians?"

"Shut up, Slim."

"But, Dewy—"

"Shut *up,* Slim."

Slim looked like he might start crying again.

"We'll do it," Dewy said after another brief bout of contemplation. "I'd rather take my chances with Indians than with Mr. Franklin."

After another blank moment or two, Slim nodded slowly. "Yeah, I do believe you're right about that, Dewy."

Fargo said, "Fine. Let me make sure you two fellows don't have any other weapons on you before I let you go."

"Ain't you even gonna leave us a knife or nothin'?" Slim looked scandalized. He cast a pleading glance at Dewy. "Ain't he gonna even leave us our knives, Dewy?"

Fargo answered the question by relieving both men of several weapons they'd had hidden on their persons. He then had a thought that would spare himself some bother. "Go inside my room and grab Mr. Pearl's feet, fellows." He peeked at the corpse and added, "Wrap him up in a blanket first. Then you can each grab a foot and drag him downstairs. I don't care to have him cluttering up my room any longer. This man"—he toed the still-unconscious form on the hallway floor—"can stay here."

He thought some more while Dewy and Slim rolled Pearl's body in a blanket, and changed his mind. "On second thought, take this fellow's clothes off before you go."

"Take his clothes off?" Slim stopped wrapping the dead man, evidently unable to move and think at the same time. He turned to Dewy. "Did he say to take his clothes off, Dewy?"

"Yes, Slim. That's what the man said."

"Take them with you," Fargo added. "I don't expect your friend here—what's his name, anyway?"

"That there's Clete," offered Slim.

"I don't expect Clete will feel much like doing anything violent if he wakes up in the middle of the street buck naked, do you?"

Slim cast a worried glance at Dewy, who only shrugged. "You got the gun, Fargo."

"You're a wise man, Dewy," replied the Trailsman.

He supervised the disrobing of Clete. He let him keep his longjohns on for propriety's sake. Then he covered Dewy and Slim with his Henry as they carried the snoozing Clete downstairs and outside. They tried to set him down on the boardwalk, but Fargo didn't let them.

"Middle of the street, boys."

They put him smack in the middle of the wide, muddy avenue. Then they went back upstairs for Pearl's corpse, which they unrolled and left beside Clete. They covered Clete with the blanket so he wouldn't freeze to death if the weather took a turn for the worse.

Fargo held his gun on the two henchmen until they'd ridden off into the night. He didn't expect they'd be back any time soon. They probably didn't fear him too much, but they had every right to worry about what Franklin would make of their botched night's work.

He knocked on Purvis's door before he went back upstairs. Purvis was rubbing his eyes when he came to open the door. He peered out at Fargo uneasily.

"Those men of Franklin's came to shoot me, and one

of them got himself killed in my room, Mr. Purvis. I'm going to move my things to the room next door if it's all right with you."

"A man got—?" Purvis gulped audibly, blinked, and muttered, "Hell. I figured it was something like that when I heard all the commotion."

Fargo nodded. "Sorry about the mess, but I was asleep when they snuck in."

Purvis heaved a gusty sigh. "Yeah. That doesn't surprise me. Franklin doesn't go in for daylight raids. He does his work like a thief in the night."

"So I've heard."

With a wave of his hand, Purvis said, "Sure, go ahead. Take any room you want. If Franklin comes here in the morning to kill me, though, I hope to God you'll tell him this wasn't any of my doing."

"Not a problem, Mr. Purvis." Fargo tipped his hat. "Thanks."

"Sure," Purvis mumbled sarcastically. "Any time."

Fargo chuckled as he climbed the stairs, collected the things he'd left in his original room, and went next door to resume his interrupted slumber.

8

Clay Franklin didn't pay a call on Skye Fargo in the morning. When Fargo awoke, the sun's rays were creeping in through the crack of window visible between the curtains. When he pulled the curtains back—standing well to one side in case anyone happened to be aiming a rifle at his window—icicles dripped from the eaves and glittered like jewels in the hard winter sunshine. He was pleased to see them, since he imagined John Henry Pearl's corpse would have kept nicely in the frigid air.

When he looked to where Slim and Dewy had left the living Clete and the dead Pearl, neither body was there. Fargo presumed Clete had managed to amble away on his own. Someone must have taken John Henry Pearl to the undertaker's, unless a pack of coyotes had come to town and dragged him off to feast upon. He suspected the former, though, under the direction of one Clay Franklin.

He made a trip out of his room to see if Joey Scarlet was still snoring at the end of the hall. He wasn't, and Fargo presumed he'd made his way back to whatever hole he'd crawled out of. He returned to his room and gazed out of his window some more.

Spanish Bend looked no different today than it had yesterday, which, to Fargo's mind, was unfortunate as it wasn't a pretty place. A few men walked along the boardwalk, hunched over and shivering in the icy wind. A buggy had drawn up in front of the local mercantile. Fargo even saw a woman, bundled in black from head to toe against the cold, walking briskly across the street in the direction of the hotel.

He squinted harder. Damn, her walk was familiar. His eyes popped open when he realized who it was.

"Kitty! What in hell are you doing here?" he muttered to himself as he grabbed his clothes and threw them on. If Franklin didn't get to her first, he might just paddle her pretty little rump for being such a damned fool as to show herself in Spanish Bend.

He was still tugging on a boot and hopping down the hall two minutes later, hoping like thunder the whole time that he'd recognized her before any of Franklin's thugs had.

She had just entered the hotel lobby when he clattered down the stairs. She gave him a smile as glorious as the dawn, but it faded into a soft screech when, without a word, he scooped her up and ran to the stairs with her.

"Skye! What the devil are you doing?"

"Trying to save your fanny, dammit! What the hell did you come to town for?"

She was wriggling like an eel in his grasp. If he wasn't so mad, he might have thought it was kind of funny. When he threw her onto his bed, he wasn't gentle about it.

"Damn you, Skye Fargo! How dare you toss me around like a sack of flour!"

"What are you doing in town?"

"I came here to help you!"

Her cheeks were pink, her hat had fallen off, her hair was a mess, and she was absolutely furious. Skye stared down at her for about ten seconds before his anger dissipated and he began to laugh. His laughter only seemed to infuriate Kitty, who swarmed up from the bed like so many angry bees, and began pounding his chest with her fists. As tough as Kitty was, she was no match for Fargo, who laughed harder, caught her wrists, and held her away from him.

"Kitty O'Malley, if you aren't the damnedest female I ever saw."

Even though she was still as angry as a charging bull, he pulled her into his arms and held her tight. Damn, he was glad to see her, if only because he knew for sure that she was still alive and well. "How'd you get here, anyway?"

She struggled for a moment or two before she finally gave up. "I rode the mule." Her words were muffled against his shirt.

"Like the Virgin Mary to Bethlehem?" Fargo jested.

"Don't you dare blaspheme in front of me, Skye Fargo!"

Skye shook his head in wonder. "I swear, Kitty, I don't think anything will ever get you down for long."

She sniffed haughtily. "You're right, damn you."

"But there's nothing you can do here. Now I'll only have to watch out for you and my own ass both. You can be a pain in the neck without half trying."

"Dammit, Skye, you don't know what you're talking about! I had to leave that blasted cabin because two of Franklin's men showed up there! I don't know what happened to them, but they didn't have any guns. It's a good thing, too, or I'd probably be dead right now!"

"My God. Slim and Dewy."

Kitty's eyes narrowed. "You know about them?"

"I'm the one who disarmed them."

She snorted. "I might have known. And after you took

away their guns, you told 'em to go to that cabin and shack up with me? What kind of friend are you, anyway?"

Fargo had started chuckling again, imagining the confrontation between the unarmed Dewy and Slim and the well-armed and extremely dangerous Kitty O'Malley. "No, I didn't tell them to go to the cabin. I didn't know they knew it was there."

"Everybody knows it's there." Kitty sounded disgusted.

"Did you shoot at them?"

"No." After a second, Kitty grinned. "But I sure as blazes scared the life out of them." Her grin vanished. "But that doesn't explain why you're manhandling me, Skyc Fargo!"

"Hell, Kitty, I'm only a man. How else am I supposed to handle an enraged woman? Anyway, I don't have time to watch out for you while I tackle Franklin and his men."

He still chuckled, but Kitty wasn't mollified. "*Damn you, Skye! You don't have to watch out for me! I can watch out for myself. I came here to help you, not be a burden!"

As much as he appreciated Kitty's spunk, Fargo thought it would be well to nip her aspirations in the bud. "What you're going to do is stay in my room out of sight."

"I'll be damned if I will!"

"If you don't, I swear to God I'll tie you to the bed and stick a gag in your mouth. You'd be a hell of a lot more comfortable if you agree to behave yourself."

"I'm not a baby!"

Despite her indignation, he was beginning to react to

her softness pressed against him, and he chuckled again. "You're sure not. You're definitely not a baby."

Kitty couldn't hold her anger against Fargo's wiles. After another moment or two of rebellion, she laughed too. "All right, I'll stay here, but I won't like it."

"Tell you what. You can keep watch out the window, and if you see anybody sneaking up on me, you can screech. That all right?"

"Humph. If I see anybody sneaking up on you, I'll shoot him from here to kingdom come."

"You're a bloodthirsty wench, Kitty O'Malley. What am I going to do with you?"

She eyed him sourly for a moment, then grinned. "I know something you can do with me." She threw her black bonnet onto the chair and unbuttoned her black coat.

Fargo's eyes popped open when he realized she wore nothing under the coat. "You must have dressed in a hurry, Kitty."

"What else could I do with those two brutes tied up in the barn, struggling to get loose? I took off my nightie, threw on my coat, and lit out of there as fast as I could."

Kitty's body was any man's dream. Her soft skin seemed to glow in the early morning light, and her curves teased him. Her breasts were works of art—big and firm and rosy-nubbed, and his groin tightened as he stared hungrily. "I'm not complaining."

"Good, because I intend to put you to some good use, Trailsman." The coat fell away from her body and she walked toward him, swaying seductively, her arms held out.

He walked into them, happy to oblige. As Kitty worked on his shirt buttons, Fargo stroked her gloriously rounded buttocks. "You're smooth as silk, Kitty, and soft as anything."

"And you're hard as iron." She stroked the bulge in his trousers, and Fargo groaned. "Here, Skye, you have too many clothes on."

She unbuttoned his buckskin breeches and pushed them down, working them past his manhood, which she took in both of her hands. "I love this thing of yours, Skye."

He gasped as her tongue ran the length of his pole. "I'm sure glad of that." His knees were about to buckle under him, so he braced himself on the bedpost and gave himself up to the pleasure of Kitty's mouth and tongue.

When he feared he was going to erupt, he panted, "Let's get on the bed, Kitty." He groaned when she let his manhood slip from her mouth.

"Come on, Skye. I need you in me. Now."

Fargo was of a like mind. He tumbled with her onto the bed. As one hand sought the curls between her legs, his mouth feasted on her breasts. Her nipples were rigid when he slid his tongue over them one at a time. She arched her hips and hissed when his thumb found the nub of her pleasure and his middle finger dipped into her hot, wet sheath.

He murmured, "You're beautiful, Kitty."

She reached for his stiff sex and stroked gently. "So are you. I need you, Skye. Now." With that, she pushed him onto his back and straddled him. He watched, fascinated as she positioned herself above him and lowered herself onto his aching shaft slowly, tantalizing them both. Her eyes closed, and she let out a sigh of pure pleasure as she buried him into her to the hilt. Fargo reached for her breasts and fondled them as she rocked on top of him, sliding him in and out in a heavenly rhythm. Fargo drew her down on top of him so that he could feel her breasts against his chest, and she pumped faster and harder until they were both in a frenzy of urgency.

He felt her stiffen on top of him and grabbed her buttocks to hold her down. She kissed him hard, sliding her tongue into his mouth to mate with his—and then it happened. With a muted shout, she achieved release. As soon as he felt her sheath begin to contract around him, Fargo gushed into her, filling her completely with his essence.

They were both dewy with sweat and drained when she collapsed onto him. "I swear, Skye, nobody makes me feel as good as you do."

Fargo was too enervated to respond in kind, although he wanted to.

Several panting minutes later, he sighed. "As much as I'd like to, I can't stay in bed with you, Kitty. I've got a town to rescue."

She sighed too. "Aw, Skye, do you have to go right now?"

He eyed her and grinned. "Yes. If I don't go now, I'll be ready for another go-round, and I'll never get out of here. You do amazing things to me, Kitty."

"That doesn't sound like such a terrible idea to me," Kitty said in her most seductive voice.

Unfortunately, her most seductive voice was one that sounded least like the Kitty O'Malley Skye Fargo knew and admired. He laughed and got out of bed. He'd already decided what he aimed to do today, and he wanted to get started as soon as possible. With luck, he'd have Spanish Bend freed from Clay Franklin's claws before nightfall.

"I forgot to ask you how Alfie is doing, Skye."

When he glanced toward the bed, Kitty looked worried.

"Alfie's fine, Kitty. He came here last night and we talked about everything."

She released a big gust of air in relief. "You sure he's all right?"

"I'm sure."

She scowled. "I could kill Franklin with my bare hands for what he did to Alfie and Sally."

As Fargo pulled on his trousers, an idea occurred to him. He said, "Tell you what, Kitty. I think you'll be able to help me after all, but it'll take some climbing."

Her eyebrows arched over her pretty blue eyes. "*Climbing?* What in blazes are you talking about?"

"I'll tell you later. I've got to get to your saloon and discuss it with a couple of other people first."

"My saloon?" Kitty brightened. "Get something for me to wear while you're there. Ask Violet. We're about the same size."

He eyed her voluptuous naked curves critically. "I don't know, Kitty. I think I like you better that way."

"I know what you like, big man, but bring me some clothes anyhow."

"All right. After I finish my business there."

"Which is?" Kitty's forehead puckered, and she looked suspicious.

"Why, I'm going to gather up some recruits, of course."

Kitty scrambled out of bed, giving Fargo a delightful look at her lush and lovely bare assets. "What the devil are you talking about?"

He buckled his holster and opened the door, grabbing his hat as he went. "You'll know soon enough. Keep out of sight until I come back. I'll try to remember to pick up some clothes for you." He winked at her.

"You bastard!" Kitty threw a shoe at him, but it only banged against the door. Fargo laughed all the way down the stairs.

As he passed the front desk, he noticed that Mr. Purvis looked a little rattled. He tipped his hat politely.

Purvis blurted out, "Mr. Fargo, did you know they found somebody passed out in the alley behind my hotel this morning? It was Joey Scarlet, and his head was busted. They had to take him to the doctor. He's stove up pretty bad, and he says he can't remember how it happened."

"Scarlet?" Fargo shook his head. "I don't believe I met him."

"No, I don't expect you did. He's another no-good one of Franklin's sons of bitches."

Fargo nodded. "I get the feeling that's one of Franklin's primary requirements."

"You got that right."

Since that required no response, Fargo gave none.

Purvis cleared his throat. "You know, Mr. Fargo, if Franklin's men keep dropping like they did last night, there won't be any of 'em left in Spanish Bend before very long."

He had such a hopeful expression on his face that Fargo couldn't help but grin. "I reckon that's so. I suppose you can always wish for the best, Mr. Purvis."

Purvis nodded slowly. "Yeah. I'll do that, all right. I'm also willing to help if anyone cares to do something that involves more than wishing for the best."

Fargo tipped his hat again. "I'll keep it in mind if I hear anything."

"Thanks."

Fargo had begun to suspect that if anyone in Spanish Bend had bothered to organize the town's merchants before this time, Clay Franklin wouldn't have been able to secure his stranglehold on the place. It would be harder to wrest the town away from him than it would have been to prevent his taking it over in the first place, but Skye didn't despair. Hell, he'd tackled harder problems in his life. Lots of times.

The wind was whipping down the dirt road as if it aimed to blow the entire community of Spanish Bend off the face of the earth. Which, all things considered, might not be such a bad idea, if it weren't for Kitty and the other people in town who'd been victimized so cruelly by Clay Franklin.

Fargo held his hat down as he glanced around, searching primarily for any of Franklin's men, but also taking note of the shoddy appearance of the place. These territorial towns would need several more years of habitation before they looked like anything resembling civilization. Fargo hoped he wouldn't be around to see it happen. He liked the wilderness and could take civilization only in small doses, and preferably with a willing woman.

The outer door of the Pecos Belle was closed against the freezing wind. Fargo opened it cautiously and peered in over the batwing doors. Nothing seemed out of place. It was around noon, and there were several men drinking at the shiny bar, several women coyly trying to earn some money from the patrons, and Alfie Doolittle, his demeanor as vapid as a cloud, grinning up a storm and pouring out whiskey. Fargo shook his head and decided he'd be glad when Alfie could be himself again, and Kitty could run her own place in peace.

He pushed through the batwings and headed for the bar, making sure he kept the entire saloon in his range of vision, either physically or reflected in the mirror behind the bar. Franklin was on his throne in the corner, presiding over his little kingdom. Fargo hoped he'd enjoy it while it lasted, because it wouldn't be his for much longer. Fargo planned on seeing to it.

"Hey there, Skye. How're ya doin'?"

Fargo squinted at Alfie, smiled, and said, "I'm doing fine, Alfie. You?"

Considering the two men had parted company only a few hours earlier, they both knew the questions and answers were meaningless, but they proceeded if only to keep up the charade.

"Fine, fine." Alfie poured bourbon into a glass for Fargo. "Whoops! Sorry, Skye. I spilled a little here." He leaned over the bar with his rag.

Fargo took the hint and leaned over too.

"The girls are ready to help any time you want 'em to, Skye. Violet's got 'em all riled up and ready to roll."

Fargo heaved a sigh. Just what he needed: a herd of wild women ready for battle. He supposed it could be worse, and he *had* asked Alfie to get their support for the upcoming transfer of power in Spanish Bend. "Thanks."

Alfie gave him a big grin. "Don't look so worried, Skye. They ain't going to do nothing until you say so. It's too important to 'em. They ain't going to interfere with your plans."

Tipping his glass toward Alfie, Fargo muttered, "Glad to hear it." He sipped his bourbon.

"Violet can fill you in on the details."

"Right. Where is she?"

As if on cue, he heard Violet's voice, hard and scared, coming from behind him. He whirled around to see what was the matter.

"Ow! Dammit, Johnny, let me go! You're hurting

90

me!" Violet looked both frightened and mad as a bee-stung cat.

A burly six-footer held Violet's wrist and leered down at her. "C'mon, Vi. I know you like it rough."

Fargo scowled. He could tell Violet didn't appreciate being mauled. He set his glass on the bar, glancing into Franklin's corner to see if he aimed to haul Johnny away from Violet. Since he had an ugly grin on his face, as if he were enjoying the show, Fargo realized Violet's rescue would probably be up to him. "Just what I need," he grumbled. "Another excuse to rile Franklin."

"Dammit, Skye," Alfie ground out between his teeth. "Franklin's men think they're kings around here, and they're brutal to the girls. It ain't fair."

"Yeah, so I see."

Violet squeaked when Johnny twisted her arm behind her back at a painful angle and drew her up against his chest.

"Stop it!" she cried.

"Hell, I just wanna have me a little fun, Vi. And you're just the girl I need to do it." Still holding her arm, he used his other hand to rake her skirt up and planted his hand on her bottom. She tried to wriggle free, but he held her too tightly.

Fargo saw that there were tears in her eyes, almost certainly from the pain. He murmured, "Cover me, Alfie," and took three giant steps toward the fracas. Out of the corner of his eye, he saw Franklin's grin turn upside down into a frown.

"Let the girl go, Johnny," he said softly. "She doesn't seem to be having any fun."

Johnny had been concentrating on feeling Violet's rear end, and he jerked his head up, obviously irked with the interruption. "Who the hell are you?"

"Name's Skye Fargo." He had his Colt out by this time.

For no more than an instant, Fargo saw fear in Johnny's face. Almost immediately insolence replaced it. "The hell you say. What in blazes are you interfering for, Fargo? I'm only having me some fun."

"The lady's not enjoying it. Let her go." Fargo gestured with his Colt. "Now."

Johnny glanced at Franklin—for direction, Fargo imagined. He didn't get it. Franklin only glowered at the scene before him.

"This ain't no lady. She's a whore, and she works here, Fargo," Johnny growled.

"It's not my job to be pawed and hurt by you, Johnny Stamp!" Violet didn't seem as afraid now that Fargo was trying to assist her.

"Shut up, Violet." Johnny twisted her arm harder, and she cried out.

"Let her go." Fargo's voice was imperative.

With a quick gesture, Johnny thrust Violet behind him. She stumbled and fetched up against a table hard, grunting in pain.

"Who the hell do you think you are, to come in here and order me around, Fargo?"

"Skye! Watch out."

Alfie's voice behind him made Fargo realize he'd made a blunder. Before he could react to the warning, he felt a blow at his back and fell forward, something as big and smelly as a grizzly clinging to his neck. He tried to hold on to the Colt, but it fell from his fingers and slid across the floor.

Violet screamed. Fargo clawed at the hands around his neck, to no avail. They tightened until his eyes were bulging and he saw spots in front of them. Of all the stupid— Furious with himself, he made a tremendous effort and got to his feet. With his last ounce of strength, he bent double and flipped his attacker over his back and onto the floor in front of him. Unfortunately, the man didn't let go, so Fargo went down with him.

It was all he could do to remain conscious during the next second or two, and when he heard an enormous boom, he wasn't sure if it was his own head pounding or an external noise until the fingers fell away from his throat. Struggling to his hands and knees, he could only pant for a moment before he shook his head to clear it and looked up.

"Holy hell." He could hardly believe his eyes. It was Violet who'd made the big noise—and she'd done it with his Colt, with which she now held Johnny Stamp at bay.

"Make one single little move, Johnny, and I'll blow you to hell, just like I did to Ralph there." Smoke curled from the end of the gun, and Violet's hand shook like a leaf in a high wind. Her voice was steady as a rock.

So Fargo had been attacked by Ralph, whoever he was. Still feeling unsteady, he rose to his feet and swallowed once or twice just to make sure he still could. Violet grinned at him. "Thanks, Mr. Fargo."

"Thank *you*, Violet."

She handed him his gun, and he took over covering Johnny. "I think you owe the lady an apology, Stamp."

Johnny snorted derisively. "That's ain't no lady. That there's a whore."

Violet's lips pinched tight. Fargo drew the hammer back on the Colt. "That's not a nice thing to say, Stamp."

Suddenly Franklin spoke from his corner. "You're a real pain in the ass, you know that, Fargo?"

"He was trying to help me, Mr. Franklin," Violet said indignantly. "Johnny was hurting me."

It looked for a moment as if Franklin wanted to set his dogs on the both of them. His lizard's eyes seemed to spit hate. But he took in a deep breath instead and said, "Yeah. That wasn't nice of him, was it?" He jerked his head at Ralph. "Is he dead?"

Ralph opportunely let out a groan just then, and Violet said, "No." She sounded disappointed.

The grin Franklin aimed at Johnny was as frozen as the weather. "You're a damned fool, Johnny. There are rooms upstairs for playing with the girls."

Violet sniffed. "He's not going to play with me anymore, Mr. Franklin. He's too mean, and he always hurts." She threw Franklin a defiant glance, which he returned with another one of his icy grins.

"Get Ralph to the doc's place, Johnny. I'll have a chat with Violet later to let her know what's expected of any female who works in my joint."

Fargo didn't like that idea. He said, "Wait a minute, Mr. Franklin. If you don't mind, I think I'll spend a little time with Violet. I'm sure she's an asset to your business. A fellow just has to treat her right, is all." He didn't holster his Colt since he didn't yet trust Johnny Stamp not to shoot him.

"That's the truth, Mr. Franklin," came Alfie's voice from behind Fargo. "Violet, she's a good girl. It's Johnny. The girls don't like him because he hurts them."

Johnny snorted, as if he'd never heard such a silly thing in his life.

"It's true, Mr. Franklin." Violet sounded as if she knew she was in for it, and was pleading. "I always try to earn my way, but I don't like to be hurt, and he was hurting me."

94

"Yeah?" Franklin looked tired of it all. "All right. You go along and play with Mr. Fargo, Violet, and let that be an end to it." He turned his head and pinned Johnny Stamp with a vicious frown. "Didn't I tell you to do something, Johnny? You'd better get at it."

Johnny didn't like it. His lips compressed, his eyebrows went down, and his cheeks got red beneath their stubble. But he did as his boss had told him, grabbing Ralph by the feet and dragging him. Alfie was right there with a mop, cleaning up the trail of blood.

Fargo heard Violet sigh with relief and finally put his gun away. Making sure Franklin was still in range of his sight, he spoke to Violet, who was pale and shaky. "Want to go upstairs, Miss Violet? I won't hurt you."

She smiled gratefully. "Thank you, Mr. Fargo." She shot an apprehensive glance at Franklin, who only nodded. "Sure. Let's go upstairs."

Fargo thought she was remarkably calm for a girl who'd just shot a man, but when she grabbed on to his arm, she was trembling. He put an arm around her and glanced at Franklin. "Sorry about the trouble, Mr. Franklin."

"Yeah, me too." Franklin swallowed the whiskey in his glass and snarled, "I don't suppose you know anything about a fellow named Joey Scarlet whose head got bashed in last night? Or John Henry Pearl, who ended up dead? Or Clete, who got laid buck naked in the middle of the street? Or Slim and Dewy, who can't be found anywhere?"

"Uh-oh." The comment came from Alfie, who'd returned from mopping up after Johnny Stamp.

"Yeah, I know about all of them, Franklin. They tried to bushwack me in my hotel room last night. You wouldn't know anything about *that,* would you?"

The two men eyed each other for several seconds, Fargo silently challenging Franklin to explain his men's behavior, Franklin glaring daggers at Fargo. At last, Franklin said, "Watch your back, Fargo. My men don't like smart asses. And *I* don't like men who try to move in on my territory."

Fargo held up a conciliatory hand. "Wouldn't dream of it, Mr. Franklin."

Franklin picked up his glass, saw that it was empty, and bellowed, "Bring me some whiskey, dammit!"

Clutching Fargo's arm tightly, Violet let out a huge sigh, and Fargo perceived that she knew the dangerous moment had passed. He glanced at Alfie, who confirmed his opinion with a brief nod and a grin.

"Come on, Violet. Let's go upstairs and get you calmed down." He signaled to Alfie, who produced a bottle of bourbon. Fargo expected Violet could use a hefty shot by this time.

As they headed up the stairs, Violet was a trifle unsteady. "I never shot nobody before," she whispered.

"I know it, honey. You just take it easy now."

By the time they got to Violet's room, she was crying, probably with relief. Fargo sat her down on the bed and poured her a good shot. With trembling hands, she lifted the glass to her lips and choked down the drink. Fargo sat in a chair and waited, knowing she needed some time. In a minute or two, her tension eased, and she looked up at him.

"Thank you. I was so scared. Johnny likes to hurt the girls. Some of them still have scars."

He shook his head. "I'm sorry you have to deal with trash like him, Violet. I'm going to try to help you out so you won't have to."

She nodded. "Alfie told us. We'll do anything you say, Mr. Fargo."

"Good. The first thing you can do is let me borrow a dress."

She stared at him, surprised, and he laughed. His explanation did a lot to wipe away the horror of Violet's last several minutes, and she agreed to take a dress over to the hotel as soon as she could. "Kitty! Oh, thank God! I've been so worried about her."

"She's fine. And you and the girls here can help get the Pecos Belle back for her."

Violet's mood lifted the rest of the way, and she was soon fit to discuss particulars with Fargo. She gave him details about the men who had been posted by Franklin to keep the town in his grip, and she agreed to prime her fellow working girls for the ultimate showdown, which Fargo expected would take place that night.

She got on her tiptoes and kissed his cheek before he left the room. "Good luck, Skye. We'll never forget how you helped us. Thank you so much."

He grinned down into her big brown, trusting eyes. "Don't thank me yet, Violet. Wait until we know if it works."

"It'll work," she said with conviction.

Fargo hoped to God she was right.

9

As soon as he shut the door to Violet's room, Fargo considered his first move. After a moment's thought, he decided to start out his mission by introducing himself to the sheriff. According to Violet and Alfie, the man was one of Franklin's minions, but it was vaguely possible that, as sheriff, he had a scruple or two to rub together. If so, he might be of use to Fargo.

He scanned the saloon as he went down the stairs, making sure that no one was waiting for him. Franklin was no longer in his corner, and there didn't appear to be any of his bodyguards around. That seemed strange to Fargo, so he visited the bar for a chat with Alfie before he ventured outside. For all he knew, there was an army of Franklin's gunsmiths out there, waiting for him.

Alfie greeted him with a full glass and a worried look on his face. "How's Violet, Skye?"

"She'll be all right. She's got a strong will and a good head on her shoulders."

Alfie was relieved. "That she has. What are you going to do now?"

"I aim to pay the sheriff a visit, but I'm wondering where Franklin is."

"He called his men together, and they're in the back room now for what he called a conference. I expect he's ripping into them good and proper. I think he's worried about you, Skye. Better watch yourself."

"I aim to." He aimed to work fast, too, before Franklin figured out what his intentions were. "What can you tell me about the sheriff?"

"Gosset?" Alfie spat at a cuspidor sitting under the bar. "He's a bastard."

Fargo sighed. "I was afraid of that."

"You going to tackle him?"

"I expect I'd better, and get it over with first."

"Yeah, you're probably right. Well, good luck."

"Thanks."

Fargo experienced no trouble leaving the saloon. Several men eyed him speculatively, but they offered no opposition. He glanced up and down the road before he pushed through the batwings. The wind was still ripping down the street like an avenging demon, and most of the citizens of Spanish Bend had gone inside to seek more congenial surroundings.

The sheriff's office was only a few doors away from the saloon. There was only one way in, and Fargo took it.

A man sat behind a dilapidated desk, dealing out a game of solitaire with a grimy deck of cards. A stove sat in a corner, radiating inadequate heat that didn't reach the windows, which had fogged over. The man looked up and scowled when the door opened and slammed his cards down onto the desk. "Skye Fargo. I heard all about you. What the hell do you want with me?"

"Just came to get acquainted, Sheriff," said Fargo as he closed the door. He smiled, trying to make his expression appear friendly. The sheriff didn't seem to be buying it, which indicated he was more astute than he looked.

"I suggest you get out of town, Mr. Fargo," he growled. "The sooner the better."

"I expect to be leaving soon, Sheriff. First, though, I wanted to chat with you about Mr. Franklin and all the so-called accidents that have been happening in Spanish Bend."

The sheriff got a squinty-eyed smirk on his face. "There ain't no accidents been going on in Spanish Bend that I can't handle, Fargo."

"That's what I figured," Fargo muttered. With one comprehensive glance around the room, he divined that the sheriff was alone in his office. That being the case, he wasted no more time on talk. Still smiling to keep the sheriff off guard, he walked to the desk, hooked his foot under a rung of the sheriff's chair and suddenly tipped him over backward.

The fellow only had time to utter one sharp "Hey!" before Fargo grabbed the dirty bandanna from around his beefy neck and stuffed it into his mouth. Although he was on his back, the sheriff groped wildly for the gun on his hip, but he had no luck.

Fargo shook his head as he yanked the sheriff to his feet. "You're no better at your job than Slim and Pearl were at theirs, Sheriff. Franklin ought to hire himself more competent men before he tries to take over any more towns."

With the gag in his mouth, the sheriff couldn't respond. Nor could he prevent Fargo from tying his hands and legs together. He grunted like a wild boar as Fargo hauled him to the office's one small cell and locked him in, taking the keys with him. As he left the office and locked the door behind him, Fargo heard the bars of the cell rattling as the sheriff threw himself against them in rage. He contemplated going back inside and knocking the man on the head so he couldn't make so much noise, but vetoed the notion. Most of Franklin's hirelings hung out at the saloon. Besides, even if someone heard the racket, chances are they wouldn't care enough—or even dare—to investigate its cause.

Another thump was followed by a crash and a muffled grunt of pain. It must be difficult for the sheriff to maneuver with his hands and feet tied. Fargo wondered why he even bothered to try.

"Idiot. He'll only bruise himself," he muttered as he glanced up the street and decided where he should go next. He wanted to work fast so as to eliminate as many hazards as possible before he and the girls and Alfie sprang their final trap. Violet had told him where Franklin's most devoted followers could be found, so he had a choice between the livery stable and the dry-goods store.

Clay Franklin cast a jaundiced eye over the men lined up in front of him. "You're a pack of blundering idiots," he told them flatly. He looked around the room. "Where the hell is Stamp?"

A couple of the men muttered that they didn't know.

Franklin didn't like that. "I told everybody to be here, dammit. Can't any of you jackasses follow instructions? Even simple ones like 'come to a meeting'?"

Several of his hired thugs shuffled their feet uncomfortably. One or two looked as if they didn't like being called jackasses and idiots, but none of them dared to object. Clay Franklin wasn't noted for indulgence toward men who bucked his authority.

Franklin continued in a voice as cold as the weather. "To hell with Stamp. This Skye Fargo is nothing but trouble, and I want him out of Spanish Bend."

"You want we should jump him?" a man with a big scar across his cheek asked.

Franklin glowered at him. "A bunch of you fools have already tried that, and failed. Anyway, I don't want him shot or jumped, because I don't want the army sending any soldiers out here to butt into my business in Spanish Bend. The army's the only law the territory's got, and as far as I'm concerned, it can stay at the forts. Besides, Fargo works for the army sometimes and they might care what happens to him."

Several men, perceiving the wisdom of Franklin's thoughts, nodded.

"I'm going to assign several of you to ride out to my ranches and bring in reinforcements. Do it now. Then, tomorrow morning we'll run him out of town. He's good, but he's not good enough to fight off a hundred men. And I sure as the devil don't want him getting the townspeople behind him and trying to take back the place."

"After we ride him out of town, I expect he can have an accident," one of Franklin's men suggested.

"I'll do the expecting around here," Franklin barked. "You're no good at it. Just get him the hell out of here and on his way. If he meets with an 'accident,' the army's sure to snoop around, and I don't want them anywhere near me or my town."

Protests and grumbles filled the room.

"I'll get rid of him for you, Mr. Franklin!"

A young man stepped forward. Franklin wasn't pleased. "Sit down, Gable. I just said I don't want him killed."

"But if it's a fair fight with witnesses, nobody can do anything about it."

Franklin snapped, "Give it up, Gable. You're not fit to go up against a man like Fargo."

The youngster bridled. Some of the men gathered around snickered, and his face turned red. Everyone who lived in Spanish Bend knew that Gable wanted to make a name for himself. He wore flashy clothes, a dapper mustache, a silver-bedecked hat and belt, and a tooled-leather holster. He fingered the holster as he frowned at his compatriots before turning back to Franklin.

"I can do it, Mr. Franklin. Give me a chance."

Clay Franklin uttered a contemptuous snort. "Forget about it, Gable. Fargo's got years of hard living and straight shooting behind him. You wouldn't stand a chance. Make your rep on somebody else."

"Sit down, Gable," another man said, not unkindly. "Mr. Franklin's doing you a favor."

Another man chuckled. "Yeah. He's keepin' you alive for a while longer."

Gable, his face beet red with anger and embarrassment, pivoted and stalked out of the room.

Franklin muttered, "Watch him, boys. He's liable to do something even stupider than the rest of you've been doing."

The men in the room laughed. Franklin stopped the laughter with a furious scowl.

10

Fargo had decided to visit the livery stable first, when an ominous click from a nearby window alerted him to impending trouble. He hurled himself sideways as a shot ripped through the howling wind and slammed into the side of the sheriff's office. Scrambling, he got to the shelter of the office doorway, drew his Colt, and tried to decide what to do now. Another shot sent him inside the office, where the sheriff was still bashing himself against the cell bars.

"Come out, Fargo! I've got you now, you bastard!"

The voice belonged to Johnny Stamp. Fargo sighed. He might have known Stamp wouldn't let his humiliation pass without an attempt at revenge. "Let it go, Stamp. There's no sense in us killing each other."

"Like hell. You got no right to come waltzing into Spanish Bend and upset everything."

The saloon doors burst open and several men emerged. Among them was Clay Franklin, who looked like an enraged bull. "What the hell's going on out here?" he bellowed. His bodyguards had their guns drawn, and they were looking around as if they couldn't wait to use them.

Fargo didn't want them to come to the sheriff's office. He called out, "It's Stamp, Franklin. He decided to gun me down."

"Where the hell are you?" Franklin hollered.

"Sheriff's office."

"Where's Gosset?"

Fargo didn't think it would be wise to say he'd tied him up and shoved him into a cell, so he called back, "I don't know."

He heard Franklin's savage grumble from where he stood. "Stamp!" Franklin shouted. "Cut it out and get over here! I'm conducting a meeting, and you're supposed to be there!"

Silence from Stamp. Fargo held his breath. Franklin bellowed again. "Stamp! If you want to keep your job, you get over here *now*! If I have to tell you again, it'll be the last time anybody tells you anything!"

Another pause, longer this time—unless it was his jangling nerves that made Fargo think so—and then Stamp's voice, surly and whiny, came to him. "All right, Mr. Franklin." He showed himself. "But I don't like it."

"I don't like it when my men give me trouble," Franklin snapped. "And you were a damned fool to treat that girl bad in the middle of a crowd, anyway."

Yeah, thought Fargo. A man should only torture girls in private. He wanted to plug both men, but knew he'd never get away with it with all of Franklin's bodyguards standing around. Getting himself killed wouldn't help Kitty's cause.

Franklin continued. "Get over here, Stamp. You're supposed to be at the meeting, and you're late. We've still got a lot of things to talk about." He turned to skewer Fargo with a cold, snake-eyed glare. "There are things going on in Spanish Bend that have to be taken care of. Soon."

That meant him, Fargo imagined, and he sighed. He watched as Franklin turned on his heel and headed back into the Pecos Belle, trailed by a dozen or more of his hired guns, then left the sheriff's office. He kept watching, though, because Stamp was lagging behind, and Fargo got a tingling sensation at the base of his spine. He braced himself.

He was right. Just before Stamp got to the batwing doors, which were swinging in and out, he swirled around, his face contorted with rage, his gun in his hand. Fargo was ready with his Colt and fired before Stamp had a chance to lift his own gun to fire. Stamp collapsed on the boardwalk with his grimace still in place, dead from a bullet to the heart.

The same men who'd only seconds earlier entered the saloon, now stampeded out of it again. Franklin stopped dead when he beheld Stamp. Fargo didn't put his Colt away, because he didn't trust any of those men.

"God damn," said one of Franklin's bodyguards. He looked up from the body to frown at Fargo. "Why'd you have to kill him?"

"He drew on me," Fargo said simply. "You'll notice I didn't shoot him in the back."

Franklin stooped over the body to inspect it. He looked up and spoke to one of his men, "Roll him over. I want to see where he was shot." Glancing up at Fargo, he said, "If I find you're lying to me, Fargo, it'll be the last lie you ever tell."

Fargo didn't bother responding. The ladies from the Pecos Belle had dashed outside to see what was going on, and now stood in a huddle, hugging themselves to keep warm. Violet was the leader of the pack. Fargo saw her face drain of color when she saw Johnny Stamp's body. She staggered a little bit, and another girl grabbed her, put an arm around her shoulder, and squeezed her.

He was pleased to see the girls tried to take care of each other.

One of the men got the toe of his boot under Stamp's body, and flipped him over onto his back. The bloodstain on his chest was plain to see. Fargo breathed a sigh of relief. Not that he didn't know the stain was there, but he didn't want there to be any question that he'd been forced to shoot.

Franklin looked up, frowned, and barked, "Take the body to the undertaker. Then get back over here. Apparently we have a lot more to talk about."

From the look he got from the king of Spanish Bend, Fargo didn't have to guess what Franklin aimed to talk about.

Fargo had no sooner turned to continue on his way to the livery stable, than a shouted command brought him up short.

"Hold it right there, Fargo!"

One of the girls huddled outside of the saloon uttered a sharp scream. "My God, Vi! It's Gable!"

"Good Lord," Violet muttered.

The batwings swished again, and there was Franklin, glowering for all he was worth at the scene before him. He snarled, "For Christ's sake, Gable, what the hell do you think you're doing?"

Fargo eyed his latest adversary, the one who'd told him to hold it. It was a boy, for the love of God, and one bent on making himself a reputation by the looks of it. Fargo sighed. He didn't need this. He held up his hands. "Don't do anything foolish, boy. I'm not your enemy."

The boy twitched his shoulders nervously. "The hell you're not. Draw."

"Gable! Cut it out!"

The boy paid no attention to Franklin's barked command.

Fargo didn't want to shoot the young pup. Exasperated by the boy's foolishness, he tried to reason with him. "I don't even know your name, son. I don't like to kill men I don't know."

The boy's hands shook. He seemed to be getting more anxious by the second. "My name's Gable. Dammit, draw!"

"Aw, for God's sake!" Franklin sounded totally disgusted.

Fargo didn't want to draw. But when Gable made a grab for the revolver in his holster, Fargo had his own gun out before the boy had cleared leather. He aimed for a leg, and Gable buckled onto the street with a cry of pain. He writhed for a minute, then seemed to get himself together enough to try to aim his Colt at Fargo again. Fargo was an old hand at this sort of thing, though, and he'd moved. By the time Gable found him again, it was too late. Fargo kicked the gun out of his hand, eliciting another pained grunt.

"You're too young for this sort of thing, boy," Fargo said sympathetically. "And it's a rotten line of work. It's bad for a man's health."

"Go to hell."

It sounded to Fargo as if Gable was trying not to cry.

Franklin stomped over to the fallen Gable and frowned down at him. "I saw it this time, Gable. It was your own damned fault. I told you not to go up against Skye Fargo."

Gable didn't say a word, but only clutched his bleeding leg.

Fargo rose. He didn't replace his Colt in its holster because he didn't trust Franklin. "I think he'll be all right with some medical attention."

Franklin frowned at Fargo, then at Gable again. "You damned idiot. I ought to let you bleed to death."

Gable's bluster had gone up in smoke. He whispered, "I'm sorry, Mr. Franklin."

"Sorry?" Franklin gestured to one of his men. "Get him to the doctor, Riley." He glanced back at Fargo. "You're getting to be a lot of trouble, Fargo. I don't like trouble in my town. I think it's time you went back to wherever you came from."

"Fort Sumner," Fargo said.

"Good place for you."

Fargo cocked his head. "Is that a threat, Mr. Franklin?"

Franklin lifted his eyebrows in mock surprise. "Good heavens, no. I'm only thinking of the health of the town. And you, of course."

"Of course."

"Let's just say that you've overstayed your welcome, Fargo. You've caused a lot of trouble in a short time, and since I'm the authority here, I'm asking you to leave. If asking doesn't work . . . Well, I'm sure it will. You're a reasonable man, from everything I've heard about you."

"I like to think so."

"Good." Franklin squinted at the sky. "Weather's getting bad again, so let's say as soon as the snow stops, you get out of Spanish Bend."

Fargo smiled amiably. "You can say anything you like, Mr. Franklin."

Franklin didn't smile back. In fact, his face flushed red. "I'm not joking, Fargo. If you value your health, get out of town as soon as you can."

Fargo saluted to let Franklin know he knew exactly what he meant.

Violet and her friend were the last to reenter the saloon. Before she went inside, Violet turned and looked at Fargo. He gave her a smile that was meant to be reassuring, but she still didn't look too happy when she and her friend went back indoors.

Recalling his mission that had been so rudely interrupted, he again headed to the livery stable, run—and formerly owned—by a fellow named Gustavson. Gustavson, like several other merchants, had tried to resist Franklin and been hurt as a result.

There was no doubt in Fargo's mind, after talking to Kitty, Alfie, and Violet, that the townsfolk were badly demoralized, but he hoped he could convince Gustavson and others that they were no longer alone in their struggle. With Fargo's arrival in town, they now had an able-bodied fighter on their side and, while there were no guarantees in life, if they pulled together behind his strong leadership, they might be able to get their town back.

After all, the girls at the Pecos Belle were willing to fight for what they wanted. Why shouldn't the town's merchants be just as willing?

There wasn't a soul to be seen on the street. The wind had tapered off by this time and no longer howled. It wasn't completely complacent, though, and still blew an icy breeze that was as silent and insidious as any deadly disease. When he glanced up, he saw that the sky had turned sullen. Gigantic black clouds had started to loom in the east. It looked like the gods were going to begin spitting snow down on Spanish Bend any minute now. Fargo yanked his hat down, his collar up, and pulled his jacket closer to his body as he approached the livery stable.

He was met at the door by two burly men who, to

judge by their clothes and demeanor, weren't stable hands. To judge by their expressions, they weren't happy to see him.

One of them barked, "You Skye Fargo?"

Fargo nodded. "That's my name. You fellows work for Mr. Franklin?"

"What's it to you?"

"Nothing. It's only that I thought Mr. Franklin had called his men to a meeting."

"What's that got to do with you?"

"Nothing."

"That's right. Now, why don't you just turn around and get out. We don't want your kind in here."

"My horse is here," Fargo said reasonably. "I came to see how he's doing."

"The hell you say."

"I don't want any trouble," Fargo told the men. "I'm just here to check on my horse."

The men had been subtly trying to fan themselves out so as to get on either side of Fargo. But Fargo saw them and was prepared when the bigger of the two men lunged at him. He lowered his head so as to butt the fellow in the gut. The man staggered backward, gagging and clutching his stomach.

The other man hollered, "Damn it, you can't do that to Bobby Joe!" before leaping at Fargo, aiming for his throat.

Both men were heavier than Fargo, and this one's bulk seemed to be carved primarily out of muscle. When he hit with all of his weight behind him, Fargo went down hard. He tried to roll away from the bigger man, but succeeded only in moving about a foot before his progress was stopped by the man grabbing one of his legs. It wasn't a smart move on his part, because that left

Fargo's other booted foot free to kick him in the head, opening up a gash above his eye.

A horse whinnied, a mule brayed, and a couple of animals were frightened into nervous shufflings. Fargo thought he heard a woman's voice, but he couldn't be sure—he couldn't make out any of her words.

The man Fargo had kicked uttered a sharp cry and released the Trailsman's leg to clutch his bleeding head. The first man, Bobby Joe, had straightened up by this time. He dove for Fargo, his face crimson with rage, his bellyache forgotten.

Skye had very little time and even less space in which to maneuver, but he managed to drive a fist into Bobby Joe's kidney, which doubled him up again and sent him reeling backward. Skye knew that, although Bobby Joe would be feeling really tender for a while, he wouldn't be permanently damaged. He only hoped he'd stay out of the way long enough for Skye to take care of his partner, who wouldn't be incapacitated by his bleeding head for very long.

He was right. No sooner had Bobby Joe uttered a strangled "Oomph" and staggered away, than his friend was on the attack once more. With a savage yell, he grabbed a pitchfork from a rack on the wall and charged at Fargo with the pitchfork poised to skewer him.

Several more horses began to object to the violence and clamor with whickers and stamping hooves. By this time, a few of them were overtly upset. When Bobby Joe's friend hollered, the horse in the closest stall, a big, glossy black, whinnied in panic, reared up and began battering the stable walls with his front hooves.

Fargo, facing a head-on charge by a pitchfork-wielding opponent, dropped to the floor and rolled out of the way. His adversary wasn't nimble enough to stop his charge, and the pitchfork tines went into the wall next to the first stall with such force that the pitchfork's handle acted like a catapult. It flung the attacker aside, and he landed halfway inside the first stall.

The stall's huge black occupant, already upset, shrieked in terror, reared back again, and brought both shod hooves down on the man's chest, crushing the life out of him.

Fargo grimaced. What a way to go. He shot a glance in the other direction to see if Bobby Joe was going to offer him any further challenge. When he saw that he wasn't, Fargo approached the stall. He grabbed the dead man by the feet and dragged him out of the stable. The horse, terror-stricken, continued to buck and rear and whinny until Fargo, speaking in soothing tones, calmed him down. The horse's eyes still rolled, but Fargo guessed the poor thing wouldn't die of fright.

Now that he had some time, he drew his Colt and aimed it at Bobby Joe, who was limp in the corner. "Hand over your weapon."

The man turned around and scowled at Fargo. His eyes were streaming, not from fright, but from the vicious kidney punch he'd sustained. He wiped his eyes and his mouth on his sleeve and snarled, "The hell I will." And, in spite of the Colt in Fargo's hand and his own debilitated condition, he drew his weapon and fired. The bullet went wide, and Fargo shot him in the gut. He went down like a felled tree.

"Lordy," Fargo muttered, amazed at the idiocy of some people.

After spending a little more time calming down the cattle, he went to work tidying up. He dragged the two bodies outside the stable. Looking up and down the road, he didn't see a soul, so he figured he'd inform the undertaker about his increased workload after he spread some straw over the bloody patches inside livery stable. Horses didn't cotton to the scent of blood. He also didn't want to shock any of the honest citizens left in Spanish Bend who might visit Gustavson's.

He'd finished this last task when he heard a timid voice from somewhere behind and above him. He spun around and looked up to find a small, pretty face surrounded by a mass of blond curls, peering down at him from the hayloft. He *had* heard a woman's voice earlier. He tipped his hat. "Hello there, ma'am."

"You're Skye Fargo, aren't you?"

He admitted that he was.

"I'd heard you were good, Mr. Fargo. I guess the folks who told me so were right. But now what's my father going to do? Franklin will kill him when he finds out what you did to those men."

Fargo straightened the kinks out of his back. "Your father is Mr. Gustavson?"

The little face nodded, setting her curls to bobbing. "He hasn't been the same since my mother died and Mr. Franklin stole his business."

"Yeah. Nobody's been the same since Franklin came to town, I reckon."

"But at least he's still alive. What's going to happen to him now?"

Fargo smiled at the girl and held a hand up to her. "Why don't you come down here, and we can talk about it."

11

The girl scooted down the ladder from the hayloft, as nimble as a mountain goat. She only came up to Fargo's shoulder. Clad in men's britches, a flannel shirt, an oversized vest, and a heavy jacket, she might have passed for a young boy except for her curves, which her masculine clothes couldn't hide.

As soon as her small feet hit the floor, she ducked her head and came toward him hesitatingly. Fargo got a funny feeling about her, as if she wasn't altogether there.

"You know my name," he said, trying to sound kind and gentle. "Will you tell me yours?"

"Ursula Gustavson."

She was as pretty as a picture in spite of her dirt-streaked face. Now that she was close enough, he could see that not only was her face dirty, her clothes odd, and her feet bare even though the weather was freezing, but her blond curls were tangled and matted, as if they hadn't had the benefit of a good brushing in recent memory. Fargo saw the girl was skittish and shy, almost shaky, from fright. How many other innocent lives had Clay Franklin and his men ruined, Fargo wondered.

It seemed to him that every hour that passed here in Spanish Bend revealed more black marks against Clay Franklin. He gestured toward the door of the stable where the two men's bodies lay. "I suppose you saw what happened?"

She nodded, but didn't reply.

"Did you know those two men?"

The girl hugged her middle tightly, as if she were trying to hold herself together. Her head jerked up and down. "Of course I knew them."

"What are their names?"

"They're Bobby Joe Billings and Ray Pitkin." A sound that might have been a nervous giggle left her pretty lips.

Fargo eyed her with some concern. "You don't sound too upset that they're dead."

"I'm not." Her aspect changed so abruptly, Fargo blinked. She suddenly turned from a pretty little girl who looked like she needed a mother's attention into a hell-cat. Her cheeks bloomed with color, her blue eyes snapped with hate, and she spat out, "I wish they were still alive so I could kill them! Slowly. I wish they'd suffered as much as they made my father and me suffer. And my mother. They should have had to pay a lot for what they did to my mother."

Then she fainted. It happened so fast, Fargo wasn't able to catch her before she hit the straw. He knelt beside her and wondered what to do now. He couldn't just leave her on the stable floor.

"What's going on in here?"

Fargo glanced up at the gruff question. A man stood in the doorway, his huge body outlined by the cold winter sun at his back. Snow had begun to fall sluggishly behind him. Fargo saw fat wet snowflakes swirl gently in the breeze and wondered how long this latest snowfall would last.

"What the hell are you doing to my daughter? Haven't you and your kind done enough to her already?"

The man's accent was thick, and his voice rang with anger. His face was red with rage, his eyes blazed with condemnation, and he had his hands bunched into fists at his side. Fargo got the impression he'd like to use them, but didn't dare.

He shook his head. "I'm not one of Franklin's men, Mr. Gustavson. My name's Skye Fargo. I just eliminated a couple of Franklin's thugs, as a matter of fact. A fellow named Bobby Joe and another one named Ray. I'm afraid your daughter saw it happen. I guess it was too much for her, and she fainted."

Gustavson squinted at him for another moment or two, then grunted. His hands unclenched as he walked over and squatted beside his daughter.

"I think she'll be all right," said Fargo. "I expect it was rough on her to see the violence."

Fargo saw that the liveryman's eyes were as blue as those of his daughter when he lifted them to him. They no longer radiated hatred, at least not directed at the Trailsman. "It ain't violence against Franklin's men that ruined her. It was what Franklin's men did to her and her ma that did that."

Mr. Gustavson lifted his daughter's body tenderly and cradled her close to his chest. "They were brutal to her, Mr. Fargo. It wasn't fair what they done to her."

"I'm sure of it."

"She's only a girl." The big man's voice broke, shaking in sorrow.

Fargo couldn't think of a thing to say.

Mr. Gustavson swallowed. "If you need help cleaning the town up, you just call on me. I'll help you get those bastards."

"Thanks. I appreciate the offer."

Holding his daughter as if she weighed nothing at all, Mr. Gustavson stared at him for another several seconds before he said in a hurt voice, "Some of us tried to stop him, you know."

Fargo nodded. "I've heard about it."

"But there were too many of them, and they have no morals. They didn't care who they hurt, and they went after the families of the men who tried to stop them. My Ursula here, she saw her mother assaulted by those bastards. Then they assaulted her. She lived. Her mother didn't."

It was painful to watch the big, vibrant man tell him such things. Tears coursed down Gustavson's cheeks and splashed onto his daughter's leather jacket.

Gustavson jerked his head toward her. "You see how she dresses? She didn't used to dress like a boy, Mr. Fargo. She used to want to be a lady until Franklin's men got a hold of her. Then she tried to hide herself, and the fact that she's a female. It just ain't fair."

"You're right." Fargo felt a little helpless himself in the presence of the liveryman's potent sorrow and anger. "I'll do what I can. I know your daughter will be all right one of these days, Mr. Gustavson."

Gustavson eyed him for another second or two, then gave him a short, sharp nod. "Yeah. Me too."

"Alfie Doolittle and the girls at the Pecos Belle and I are hoping to give Franklin and his men a fight tonight at the saloon. If you can recruit some of the men in town, maybe you can back us up."

For the first time since Gustavson entered the stable, he looked interested in something besides his daughter. "What time?"

"Miss Kitty and I will be there at eight. It'll take a

while to get organized. If you and a few other men could show up outside the front door of the saloon at nine, armed, you might be a big help."

Gustavson considered it for a minute, then nodded again. "I'll be there." Then he bore Ursula off, presumably to his house.

Fargo watched him go, wrath churning in his chest. He tamped it down, knowing he had to keep his head or he'd be of no use to anyone.

Since the undertaker's place was only a couple of steps down the road, Fargo went there to inform the man he had more business stacked up outside of Gustavson's Livery Stable. The undertaker wasn't happy about the upsurge in his business, but he agreed to take care of the two bodies.

The snow that had been falling gently a few minutes earlier was now a veritable blizzard. Fargo headed back to his hotel room to let Kitty know they might have help with their fight come the night. The wind had started howling again and nearly carried his hat away. He slammed his hand down over it as he opened the hotel door.

Mr. Purvis greeted him with more cheer than he had thus far exhibited. "I heard what you've been doing today, Mr. Fargo. Thanks. Thanks a lot. Anything I can do, you just let me know."

Fargo considered the hotel keeper's offer. This was the second one. "Can you handle a gun?"

"A gun?" Purvis gulped. "I have one. I reckon I can shoot it if I have to. Don't know how good my aim is."

Fargo nodded. "I don't expect you'll have to do too much shooting. You can help if you'll keep quiet about it."

"Don't worry. I won't tell a soul unless it's other folks in town who can help us."

Fargo told him to meet Mr. Gustavson at the livery stable at eight that evening, and to await events. "You'll hear when things start happening at the Pecos Belle," he said. "Wait until then."

"Good. I hope you kill all them bastards."

"If I don't kill them all, I imagine I'll be able to persuade them to leave Spanish Bend."

It looked to him as if Mr. Purvis hoped for a more bloodthirsty answer to the problems of Spanish Bend, but he figured that was only because Purvis hadn't been involved in many deadly encounters in his life. He saluted the hotel man and hurried up the stairs to his room, praying that Kitty would still be there. As much as he admired her, he wasn't sure she'd do as he'd asked. Kitty sometimes equated common sense with boredom.

His relief, therefore, was immense when he pushed the door open and was met by Kitty's body, which she hurled at him.

"Skye! Oh, Skye, you're so wonderful!"

"Thanks, Kitty." He grinned and kissed her thoroughly. He didn't allow himself to get too distracted, though, because they still had lots of work to do.

He discussed the evening's plan with Kitty, who at one point frowned savagely. "Hell's bells, Skye Fargo! I've never worn men's britches in my entire life, and I don't intend to start wearing them now!"

"It's only for one evening, Kitty, and it's only so you can climb the rope to Violet's room without getting your feet tangled in your petticoats and breaking your neck."

Kitty scowled at him for another thirty seconds or so. Then she gave it up and favored him with a smile.

"Dammit, Skye, I can't not do what you tell me to, no matter how crack-brained your notions are."

He smiled back. "Thanks, Kitty. I knew you were a gem."

She eyed him doubtfully. "Are you sure Violet knows what to do?" She backed away from him and twirled, holding out her skirt. "She sent me this dress. Like it? Amanda brought it."

"So I see. Looks good." She looked better naked, but the dress was all right. "Anyway, Violet and I talked about it this morning. She knows, and she's ready."

"And Alfie? Is he all right, Skye?" Her face took on a beseeching expression. "I don't know why it is, but Alfie's always been kind of like a father to me, probably because I never knew my own father. If Franklin's men hurt him permanently, I don't know what I'll do."

"Alfie's fine, Kitty."

"Thank God. I've been so worried about him."

Fargo thought it was interesting that Alfie and Kitty had found each other. They made a good family for each other.

Kitty put on a mock pout and balanced her hands on her hips. "I'm starving to death, Skye Fargo. If you want me to climb up ropes, you'd better feed me first."

"I'll feed you, all right." He waggled his eyebrows at her.

She smacked him on the arm. "That's not what I mean, and you know it." She giggled.

"All right. If you're going to be mean to me, I reckon I'd better get something for us to eat." He wasn't sure how he could scare up some grub, since he didn't like the idea of wandering around Spanish Bend in plain sight, making a target of himself. "I reckon I can get something at the grocer's down the road."

Kitty thought it over. "Yeah. I reckon you can. Mr. Dillard, he was always a friend to me and the girls."

That was a hopeful thought. "Be back soon."

The wind hadn't slackened any in the short time Skye had been in the hotel room. It sliced down the straight main road of Spanish Bend like cold steel, driving sleet and snow before it. Fargo pulled his collar up, hunched his shoulders, and walked the few yards to the grocer's, trying at the same time to keep his eyes peeled for any of Franklin's men who might, like the hapless Gable, be hoping to make a name for themselves.

The weather was too rough even for hardcases, though, and nobody tried to impede his progress. When he pushed the door open, stepping out from the blast of cold winter wind, a pleasant aroma of wood smoke and spices scented the air in the small grocery. The room was as warm as the outdoors was frigid.

As soon as he lifted his head to appreciate the heady smells, however, a rude surprise met his gaze. Two men whom Fargo had last seen hovering around Clay Franklin now sat beside a stove. They looked up from their seats and stared straight at Fargo. They didn't seem surprised to see him.

He sighed and decided he should have expected it. It was too damned cold even for a villain to hang around out-of-doors. He should have known they'd seek shelter. Like rats gathering in packs around garbage dumps, Franklin's men huddled together in warm places.

One of them spat, missing the cuspidor set out for such purposes by a good six inches. "Well, looky who's here, Jim."

Jim, whose round head was as bald as a bullet, grinned, revealing a set of choppers that looked more like broken pickets than teeth. "I see him, Shep. If it ain't Mr. Skye Fargo in the flesh. I thought Mr. Franklin told you to get out of town, Fargo. Don't you hear good?" He was a bulky man and not tall. He looked like he'd be slow to think and slower to move.

Because he didn't want any trouble with these two, Fargo didn't react with hostility. "Mr. Franklin said I could wait until the weather clears, boys."

"Did he now?" Shep didn't appear pleased with the reminder. "And what if we don't want your kind here until then, eh?"

Fargo heaved an internal sigh and spared a moment to be glad he hadn't put on his gloves, even though his fingers were protesting from being exposed to the frigid weather. If he had to draw fast, frozen fingers wouldn't be as much of an impediment as his gloves would be. "Listen, fellows, I just came in for some food. Where's Mr. Dillard?"

Shep twitched his head in what Fargo assumed was a gesture indicating the rear of the store. "He's in the back room. Why don't you go on back there and talk to him?"

"Thanks. I'll wait here." He'd as soon turn his back on a crouched cougar as one of these men.

Jim snickered. "I don't think the man trusts us, Shep."

"I think you're right, Jim." Shep's expression was as cocky as a banty rooster's. "And I think he's smart not to. What do you think, Jim?"

"I think you're right, Shep."

"It's nice that you two seem to agree on things." Fargo spoke mildly, wondering which one of these characters was going to try the first move.

He didn't have long to wonder. With a speed surprising in someone who looked so clumsy, the man named Jim flipped his hand up, sending a bowie knife hurtling at Fargo, who skipped aside barely in time to avoid being skewered. As it was, the knife ripped a path through his jacket. His Colt thundered in the confined space, sending Jim and his chair tumbling over backward. Black smoke curled up from the gun and the scent of gunpowder mingled with the spicy aroma of the store.

Shep wasn't quick enough to draw. He sat still, gaping at his dead comrade. "Jeeze."

Since Shep didn't seem to be reaching for his sidearm, Fargo gave him the benefit of the doubt. He didn't take his eyes from him, however, when he knelt to pick up the Arkansas toothpick, which had clattered to the floor beside him. Damn, he liked this jacket. He wondered if Kitty would mind sewing up the rip for him. "You're a witness, Shep. He threw at me before I drew on him."

"I saw it too, Mr. Fargo," came a new and faintly shaky voice. "I saw the whole thing." The man who belonged to the voice peeked timidly around the jamb of the door leading to the back room.

"You Mr. Dillard?" Fargo didn't put down his Colt, nor did he let his attention wander from Shep, who looked tolerably more dangerous than the grocer.

The man nodded. "I—I'm Dillard. And you're Skye Fargo?"

Fargo nodded. "Sorry about the disturbance. I just came in to get some grub."

Dillard deserted the doorjamb and walked into his store. "It wasn't your fault." As he spoke, he stared defiantly at Shep, who frowned back. "Jim always was a hothead."

"I think you'd better go report to Mr. Franklin, Shep.

Tell the truth, because Mr. Dillard saw what happened too."

Shep groaned as he rose from his chair. "I'll tell the truth, damn you. The truth is you don't belong in Spanish Bend, and the sooner you get out, the better off we'll all be."

Fargo saw Dillard's lips tighten, as if he'd like to set Shep straight on a few things but was too prudent to do so.

"That's fine, Shep," Fargo said. "As long as you leave Mr. Dillard's store without any more fuss."

Shep said in a surly voice, "I didn't cause no trouble."

"True enough," Fargo agreed.

He could tell Dillard was holding his breath as Shep sauntered across the floor and went out the door.

"Do you think he'll be back, Mr. Fargo?" Dillard's voice shook again.

"I don't think so. I have a feeling Mr. Franklin's not going to be happy about another one of his men getting killed."

Dillard shuddered. "I've never seen anything like the way this town's gone straight to hell since Franklin got here." The grocer eyed Fargo closely. "Purvis tells me you aim to do something about it."

"Word gets around." Fargo grinned. "If you want to help, you can go to Gustavson's Livery Stable tonight around eight. Armed. Gustavson and Purvis will explain things to you."

Dillard seemed to waver for a moment, then said, "I'll do it!" with such vehemence that Fargo was taken slightly aback.

He said merely, "Good. I hope we can solve everybody's problems tonight. In the meantime, I've got to get something to eat or I'll fade away to a wisp and won't be able to do anything at all."

Dillard seemed happy to have been given a task he understood. "Sure thing, Mr. Fargo. I'll pack you up some fine grub. No charge."

"Thanks a lot."

Before Dillard had finished his task, two of Franklin's men arrived to haul Jim's body out of the grocery and over to the undertaker. Fargo watched from the counter, keenly aware that either one of them could draw on him if they were so inclined.

Evidently, however, Clay Franklin had lectured them sufficiently. Neither man tried to draw, although one of them grumbled, "Mr. Franklin ain't happy about this, Fargo. He says you've done a lot of damage in Spanish Bend, and he wants you out. Quick."

Fargo nodded. "As soon as the weather clears, Mr. Franklin won't ever be troubled with me again."

The man eyed him suspiciously, but only said, "Good thing that is."

Fargo silently agreed.

Dillard returned from his back room a few minutes later, carrying a big package. He looked very relieved to see the dead man gone from his floor. A big patch of blood marked the spot where he'd died. Holding the bundle, Dillard looked at the patch and grunted. "Reckon I'd better get a pail and mop. It's too damned cold for this sort of thing."

Fargo returned to his hotel room about five minutes later, laden with a wheel of cheese, some good country ham, a tub of butter, and two loaves of crusty bread.

The wind had taken to screaming in rage by this time, and Fargo had a hard job of it to get the hotel door opened with his hands full. He managed, though, and was greeted by Kitty with a big hug and a kiss when he made it upstairs to his room.

"Damn, Skye, I thought you'd run out on me."

"Had a little trouble at the grocery."

Kitty stopped still and looked up at him with huge, frightened eyes. "Franklin?"

"Two of his men. Fellow named Shep and one named Jim."

She grimaced. "Yeah, I know those two. Wicked men, both of them."

"Only one of them now."

"Why didn't you kill 'em both while you were at it?"

Fargo shook his head and grinned. The nicest people could get bloodthirsty without half trying. A knock resounded at the door, and he and Kitty exchanged a startled glance.

"Hell, Skye, I'd better hide. I don't want anyone to know I'm here."

"Good idea."

While Kitty hid behind the bed, Fargo went to the door. Standing beside it with his back to the wall, he pulled his Colt, and held it at his side. "Who's there?"

"It's Purvis, Mr. Fargo. I thought you might like something to eat. My wife and me, well, we appreciate what you're trying to do in town."

"That's nice of you, Mr. Purvis. Thanks."

He reached over, turned the door handle, and pushed the door open. The smell reached him before Mr. Purvis, looking puzzled, entered, peering around as if he couldn't figure out who had opened the door. He held a tray loaded with food in his hands.

"You alone?" Skye said from beside the door, making Purvis jump in surprise.

The hotel clerk turned and blinked at him. "I'm alone,

Mr. Fargo. And I'm not about to do anything to hurt you." He sounded a little hurt.

Reholstering his Colt, Fargo said, "Thanks, Mr. Purvis. I don't want to let my guard down yet. Not until Franklin's out of town for good."

"Reckon I can understand that." Purvis's glance fell to the tray. "Er, I hope you like this. My wife, she's a pretty good cook. She fixed you up some meat and pickles and potatoes and such-like."

"It sure smells good. Please give her my best regards." He drew a coin out of his pocket, but before he could hand it to the hotel man, Purvis shook his head.

"No, sir, Mr. Fargo, I'm not going to take your money. Hell, if you finish what you started, you'll be giving us our town back. If that doesn't deserve a meal or two, I don't know what does."

"Thanks." Fargo's stomach took that opportunity to growl in anticipation. It needed filling badly. He took the tray from Purvis's hands and set it on the night table next to the bed. "I appreciate it."

"It's nothing." Purvis rubbed his hands on his trousers and shuffled nervously. "Ah, Mr. Fargo?"

"Yes?"

"I'm not . . . well, you know, hang it, I'm an innkeeper. I'm no gunman, but I'm going to Gustavson's tonight, and I aim to help out all I can. Me and my wife both."

"Thanks, Mr. Purvis."

Fargo was touched by the gallantry of the merchants in Spanish Bend. He wished, for their sake, that someone had tried to organize an effort to defend against Clay Franklin before now. However, he was beginning to believe that taking Spanish Bend from Clay Franklin wasn't going to be as much of a bother as he'd originally thought.

He and Kitty whiled away the remaining hours of daylight with a feast of bread and ham and cheese and Mrs. Purvis's fine cooking.

12

"Dammit, these don't fit!"

Skye Fargo had been watching Kitty struggle into an extra pair of his trousers with a good deal of interest. Her plump pink bottom didn't seem to want to be squeezed quite so tightly, but she made a fine show of trying to make it fit into the confines of his britches anyway.

As it was, he merely said, "Keep trying, Kitty. You'll never be able to climb a rope in your skirt, and we've got to get to the Pecos Belle by eight o'clock, because that's when Violet's going to let the rope down. She can't leave it dangling in the wind because your butt's too big for my britches."

She threw a shoe at him. He laughed and dodged it. He wasn't quite as relaxed about the night's planned project as he wanted Kitty to believe. In truth, he'd noticed a good deal of activity transpiring across the street at the saloon, and he feared it boded ill for their upcoming enterprise.

Several men had arrived in bunches of twos and threes. Fargo suspected they'd been called into town by Clay Franklin, who intended to make sure Fargo left Spanish Bend at the earliest opportunity, whether he wanted to or not, and with an escort if necessary.

Fargo pulled the curtain aside and peered at the saloon

again. Through the howling wind and swirling snow, in the light of the lantern swaying outside the Pecos Belle, he saw three more men dismounting. They looked every bit as unsavory as those generally hired by Franklin.

"I swear I'll never wear britches again as long as I live," Kitty muttered savagely.

When he glanced at her, she'd finally managed to wiggle his trousers up over her hips. But now she couldn't button them. He grinned at her and enjoyed the show. "I'm sure all the men you meet will be happy to hear it. Alfie's going to help us tonight. He's got the girls primed and ready."

"Good for Alfie. He always was smart as anything. I knew he'd help us." Kitty's approving smile ably conveyed her confidence in the faithful barkeep.

"I only hope he doesn't use too much laudanum. Franklin's sure to get wise if all of his men keep sleeping on the job."

"Laudanum? What the devil are you talking about, Skye?" Kitty hopped on one foot and then the other as she struggled with Fargo's trousers buttons. "Dammit, I never have any trouble unbuttoning these things. I didn't know they were so hard to button up again."

Fargo smiled, enjoying the show. "He's been slipping laudanum into drinks at times. But I hope he doesn't overdo it."

Kitty paused in her efforts, and her face clouded. "Lordy, Skye, I don't want anything to happen to Alfie. I've caused him too much trouble already."

"None of this is your fault, Kitty, and stop thinking it is. And don't worry about Alfie. You're right about him being smart. He knows how to take care of himself. He'll be able to tell if anything starts to go wrong."

"I hope to God you're right."

"I am."

"So you say." After a struggle, Kitty finally managed to get the top button buttoned. She released a gigantic breath in a loud huff. "Hell, Skye, I don't know how you fellows manage to get around in these things. I can hardly breathe."

"We're built different than you are, Kitty," he said with the utmost appreciation for the differences.

"Yeah, you got that right." Kitty grabbed his old plaid flannel shirt that she aimed to wear that night. "But I'm still worried about Alfie. Even if he can tell if things start to go wrong, what can he do about them? There's only one of him, and Franklin has a whole army of villains."

"You said yourself that he knows how to use a gun. Don't underestimate Alfie. He's survived so far, and he knows all of Franklin's tricks. He's been working for him ever since you got kicked out of town, and he's seen it all."

"I did *not* get kicked out of town," Kitty told him in an offended tone. "I left on my own."

Skye rolled his eyes. "Whatever you say, Kitty."

"But I suppose you're right about Alfie." She frowned when she realized her shirttail was hanging down to her knees. "Aw, hell, now I've got to undo the pants and stuff the tail in. I'll never get the blasted things buttoned up again."

Skye chuckled. "Why don't you just tie the shirt at your waist. It'll save stuffing."

She eyed him slantways. "Save stuffing, will it? I don't know that I want to save *all* the stuffing, Skye Fargo."

He dropped the curtain. "I'm talking about the shirt, Kitty. You sure are a single-minded female."

"Humph. Look who's talking." She took his suggestion, though, and tied the shirttails into a knot at her waist. She grabbed the jacket he'd laid out for her and jammed her arms into it. The sleeves hung well down past her fingertips. "Shoot, I don't know how you expect me to climb a rope in this thing."

He considered the problem. "Here. Let me see if I can roll up the sleeves. It'll be bulky that way, but you'd better wear it because it's snowing fit to kill out there and the wind's fierce. You'd freeze solid before you got up the rope if you don't wear a jacket. Maybe you can wrap a belt around it so it won't flop around."

She took his suggestion and wrapped one of his belts over the jacket. It wound around her waist twice. Fargo didn't laugh, but he wanted to. She looked for all the world like a little kid bundled up to go outside and play in the snow. He hoped she wouldn't notice how hard he was fighting his amusement.

"All right, what else?"

"Better wear these. It's a regular blizzard." He held out a pair of his gloves.

She wasn't thrilled with Fargo's weather report, and eyed his gloves dubiously. "I've got some gloves. They aren't as thick as those, but I'll have a better grip with them than with any of yours. They're too big. Mine are wool, and they'll stick to the rope, I hope."

Kitty sat on the bed and grunted as she reached for a pair of thick socks and tugged them on. "Dammit, I can't hardly bend in the middle with these pants of yours on."

"You won't have to wear them long. As soon as we get rid of Franklin, I'll take 'em off you."

She grinned up at him. "I'll take that as a promise."

After wrestling the heavy shoes on over her thick socks and tying the laces, Kitty got up from the bed and pressed a hand to her stomach as if it hurt from being confined by Fargo's trousers. She grabbed a scarf from the night table, wrapped it over her head, covering her ears, tied it under her chin, and said, "Is it time?"

"Yeah. Just about. It's a regular blizzard out there."

She didn't sound happy as she stood with her arms held out to her sides as if she couldn't move them very well.

"Here." Fargo handed her the gun he'd just loaded. "Put this in your pocket and don't use it unless you have to."

"I won't. I've got my belly gun in my other pocket."

He nodded. "Good. Do you know if your girls have weapons?"

"If Violet's got half the brains I think she has, she's made sure they know exactly what's going to happen and when. I'm sure she's already taken steps to be sure they're prepared. They'll be armed." The grin she favored him with was purely wicked. "With luck, and if Alfie's laudanum works, they'll have most of the weapons Franklin's men usually wear."

He nodded, pleased. "True."

She took as deep a breath as her restrictive clothing would allow. "Let's get it done."

"All right." He patted the Colt in his holster, picked up his Henry, and led Kitty out the door. He hoped like thunder that Violet hadn't been delayed by anything unexpected, because he and Kitty wouldn't be able to stand around waiting indefinitely for the rope to fall. They'd freeze into solid lumps.

Mr. Purvis was dozing behind the registration desk when they descended the stairs. His eyes nearly popped from his head when he looked up and saw Kitty.

"Miss O'Malley! I didn't know you were back in

town." He clearly didn't know she'd taken to wearing men's clothes, either, because his gaze raked her from top to bottom and back again. He fairly goggled at her.

"Shhh," warned Kitty. "We don't want anyone to know I'm here. I'm gonna help Skye get rid of Franklin."

Purvis's mouth snapped shut. "You are? A woman?"

Kitty frowned at him. "Yes, I am. A woman."

Purvis swallowed.

"We're off to the Pecos Belle right now," said Fargo. "Mr. Dillard will be one of the folks gathering at Gustavson's this evening."

Kitty decided to give up her indignation and winked at the innkeeper. "It'll be drinks on the house after we get rid of Franklin and his men, Mr. Purvis."

"I see. All right, I'll do my part." Purvis swallowed again. "I'm afraid I'm not much good with a gun."

"Just point it at one of Franklin's skunks and try to look fierce," Kitty suggested.

Fargo swatted her bottom, but she didn't even feel it through the layers of clothes she wore.

Purvis nodded. Fargo didn't like the expression on his face, which had gone faintly green. He hoped to hell the man wouldn't faint when the crisis came. He didn't want to have to pamper any of the citizens of Spanish Bend tonight, because he expected to have enough trouble taking care of Franklin's mob.

The wind tore the hotel door from Kitty's hand when she opened it and slammed it against the wall of the building. The wind was so loud, they barely heard the crash. "Criminy! You warned me, I guess, but I didn't expect it to be this bad."

"It's bad, all right, but that might work to our advantage."

135

She tipped her head back and squinted at him doubtfully through the falling snow. "You think so, do you?"

"Sure. The bad guys won't be hanging around outside with the weather so cold."

"But neither will the good guys."

"You can thank your stars for that. We don't need any innocent townspeople who aren't in on the action getting in the way and getting themselves killed. We'll have enough trouble taking care of Franklin's men."

She still seemed unsure. "If you say so, Skye."

He gave her a quick hug. "You're a game girl, Kitty."

The night was too dark and the weather too miserable for him to tell for sure, but he thought she might have blushed. They had to fight the wind and snow as they made their way to the back of the saloon. Snow had already piled up in drifts against the building, and Kitty slipped on a patch of ice, but they finally reached the spot underneath Violet's window where the rope was supposed to be hanging. It wasn't. There were, however, several articles of clothing lying there. Fargo toed them with his boot, wondering whose they were and why they were there. They looked like men's duds. He didn't spend much time pondering the pile of clothes, however. He needed the blasted rope.

"Hell." He peered up at the window, which barely showed through the storm. There were candles lit inside; he could tell that much by the yellow glow emanating from within.

As he watched, wondering what was keeping Violet, the window went up. He held his breath for a second or two, and released it when he saw Violet's pretty face peering down over the windowsill. She must have seen them, because she waved once and a heavy rope followed immediately, cascading down through the snow, swinging wildly in the wind. He caught the rope and steadied it, inspecting it closely.

"God bless her, she knotted it just the way I told her to."

Kitty eyed the rope with distinct skepticism. "You mean I gotta climb up that thing?"

"You can do it, Kitty. See? She put big knots in it so you can brace your feet on them."

"Who the hell are you trying to kid, Skye?"

"Nobody. Especially not you. Come on, Kitty, you can do it. Just pretend the knots are stairs."

"St—stairs?" Her teeth had begun to chatter. Fargo knew he had to get her going, or her joints would freeze up on her, and she'd never make it to Violet's room.

"Hurry up," came Violet's hissing whisper, barely audible over the roar of the wind. "It's cold with the window open, and I don't want to freeze."

Fargo tilted his head back and peered up at her. "Everything all right up there?"

She nodded. "I had a little trouble at first, but I think it's going to be all right."

"Shoot." Kitty's voice was brittle with cold.

"Come on, Kitty. I'll give you a boost."

Good old Kitty, as dauntless a girl as Skye Fargo had ever known, clutched the rope and began pulling herself up.

"I never climbed any stairs that wiggled before," she muttered.

"I'm holding it as tight as I can."

She grunted and heaved herself up another knot.

He held his breath, hoping her hands and feet weren't too cold and stiff to secure her grip. He stood under the window and silently encouraged her up the rope. Her heavy shoes banged against the walls as she braced herself by her feet, and he decided again that he was glad for the lousy weather, even if it did make Kitty's job a little harder. If it weren't for the wind, the folks inside the saloon would surely have been able to hear the clatter she made as she slowly inched her way up the side of the building.

After the first couple of knots, she cursed the whole way up. Fargo could hardly hear her by the time she was halfway there, but he grinned and watched and finally let out his breath when he saw Violet reach out and grab at her sleeves.

"Come on, Kitty, you can do it," Violet urged.

"God damn son of a bitch," Kitty growled back.

Fargo shook his head in appreciation. "Good girls," he mumbled into the wind. After kicking furiously for a couple of seconds, her feet disappeared from his sight. He barely heard the thump Kitty's body made as it hit Violet's floor. He did hear the violent curse she uttered, but it only made him smile wider.

It was his turn now. He hoped Violet had secured the rope to something solid, because he was a hell of a lot heavier than Kitty.

She had. He hauled himself up in a third of the time it had taken Kitty, in spite of the awkwardness of having to hold the Henry as he climbed. Once he was at the window, Violet didn't need to yank him inside as he managed on his own.

"Dammit, Skye, that hurt."

He pulled the rope into the room and looked over his shoulder at Kitty, who was rubbing her aching arms. He winked at her. "You did fine, Kitty."

"Fine, my ass."

It was while he was coiling the rope that he noticed

the body on the bed. Startled, he stopped coiling for a second and stared.

Whoever he was, he was as hairy as a goat and as big as a barn. It looked to Skye as if he'd been aiming to put Violet to some good use before whatever it was happened to him, because he was buck naked. Skye glanced from the man, trussed up like a Christmas goose, to Violet, who looked proud of herself. Another glimpse at the body showed him that the fellow's manhood was lying limply against his leg and had a blue bow tied around it. "Good God." That explained the clothes underneath the window, he reckoned.

Violet sniffed and jerked a nod at the man on the bed. "That there's Benny Applegate. He thought he was going to have a good time with me tonight, but he fell asleep before he could do anything at all. The dirty skunk. He's one of the mean ones."

"God bless Alfie," murmured Kitty. She yanked off her gloves, unbuttoned the oversized jacket, and tossed it onto a chair next to a night table.

Fargo walked over to the bed and gestured at the blue bow tied around Benny's member. "Alfie didn't do that."

"I did," Violet said with a toss of her head. "Damn fool thinks his thing is something special. I figured if his thing was so special, he ought to treat it special."

Skye wondered if he should cover the man with Kitty's jacket and decided not to. If Benny awoke before the fun was over, and if he managed to get himself untied, he would undoubtedly be reluctant to enter the fray naked. Fargo aimed to give Franklin as few advantages as he could. He checked to make sure his bonds were tied tightly.

"I presume those are his clothes in the snow under your window?"

"You bet your butt they are."

"Aha." Fargo shook his head. "Remind me never to get on your bad side, Violet."

Kitty laughed.

Violet blushed. "You won't, Mr. Fargo. You couldn't."

Fargo wasn't sure about that, but he didn't argue with her. "You know how many other men's drinks Alfie drugged?"

She shook her head. "No, but I think Julie and Amanda and the other girls are down there helping him. They've been teasing Franklin's men all night, trying to get them to drink as much as they can."

"God bless Julie and Amanda, too," murmured Kitty.

Violet grabbed Fargo's arm. "But Franklin suspects something. He's been mean as a snake and as edgy as a frog on a hot rock all night. Plus, he isn't drinking anything but water. He's just sitting in his corner and glaring at everybody as if he suspects them all."

"Suspicious bastard," Kitty said, offended.

Fargo grinned. "But he's right to be, Kitty."

"Yeah, but he doesn't know it."

"True, but the way his men have been behaving all day long, I'd be more surprised if he didn't suspect something was up."

Kitty snorted. Violet started to wring her hands, then suddenly squared her shoulders. "Dammit, I won't let myself be scared until everything's over. Then I won't have to be scared ever again." Her beaming smile shattered her nervous countenance.

"Good girl." Fargo gave her an approving nod as he reached for what he assumed was Benny's weapon, a clumsy old Colt. He eyed it with some surprise. "Lord, this must be one of the originals. How'd he stay alive for so long using this thing?"

Violet sniffed. "He's proud of that too. Said it belonged to his daddy, who worked for the Patent Arms Company in New Jersey before it went bust."

Fargo glanced at Benny Applegate, thinking there was no accounting for taste. As much as he himself appreciated sentiment, he'd as soon have a weapon that had a range greater than twenty-five or thirty yards. He checked to see that the old Colt was loaded and handed it to Violet. "Try not to use this unless you're standing right next to your target, Violet. The thing's no good from far away."

She took it between two fingers, wrinkling her nose. "I expect it'd smash a fellow's head in if I used it like a club." She demonstrated by holding it by the barrel and swinging it down on the bed. It barely missed Benny's head, and Fargo shuddered. He'd had no idea the girl could be so savage.

"I expect it would," he said.

Kitty laughed. He eyed her askance. Shoot, but women surely could be heartless creatures when provoked.

"All right. Let's see what's going on downstairs."

The women looked at each other, and then back at Fargo, and they nodded in unison.

13

Violet went out first in order to check the rest of the rooms upstairs and make sure none of Franklin's men were in them and awake. After a quick survey, she gestured for Fargo and Kitty to follow her. "All clear. There's one man up here, but he's out as cold as Benny."

Fargo nodded at her and took Kitty's hand to lead her to the top of the stairs. As Violet went down the stairs to gather her troops, he and Kitty flattened themselves on the floor and peered over the banister.

Kitty frowned. "Jeeze, I was hoping more of them would be sleeping."

"So was I." Fargo pondered the goings-on below. "I reckon Alfie didn't want to make anyone suspicious."

"Hell, Skye, it wouldn't matter if they were suspicious if they all fell over and went to sleep."

Fargo chuckled softly. He saw Alfie at the bar, acting stupid and grinning at customers, and he saw Franklin in his corner. To judge from his sour expression, he was in a really bad mood. Two women, a dark-haired one and a blonde, looked as if they were trying to tease him out of his grump. The blonde picked up a glass and gestured at him with it.

"Dammit, stop that!" Franklin bellowed suddenly. He slapped the blonde hard across the face. "I told you I don't want any whiskey!"

The glass went flying out of her hand, and she pressed her fingers to her stinging cheek. Fargo could see even from where he lay that her eyes were watering from the severity of the blow.

"Damn the bastard," Kitty murmured. "I hate him."

"Can't say that I blame you," muttered Fargo. "Which girl's that?"

"Amanda," said Kitty. "She's a sweetie."

In a shaky voice, Amanda said, "I'm sorry, Mr. Franklin."

"You should be sorry," Franklin snarled. "Get me another glass of water and quit trying to be funny."

Amanda went off to do his bidding. Her cheek was as red as fire where Franklin had hit her. Violet, who had been watching from the foot of the stairs, went to her, took her arm, and whispered something in her ear. Fargo saw Amanda shoot a quick glance at the stairway and look away again just as quickly when Violet pinched her arm.

The two women separated, and Amanda continued on her way to the bar while Violet walked up to a group of men surrounding another woman. They were standing directly beneath Kitty and Fargo's perch near the stairs. She sashayed into the thick of the group, teasing the men as she did so and making them laugh. "Come with me a minute, Susie. I've got to show you something."

"Hey," one of the men said. "We was having fun. Don't go off yet."

His words were thick, a circumstance Fargo presumed was a result of whiskey dosed liberally with Alfie's laudanum bottle. He whispered to Kitty, "I think we're going to be all right tonight."

"I hope you're right."

So did he.

"I'll be right back," Susie said, patting the man's stubbly cheek.

He grabbed her by the arm and jerked her to his chest, but she maneuvered away from him with a kiss and a promise that Fargo couldn't hear from where he lay, but which the man seemed to find appealing. He raised his eyebrows, rubbed his crotch, said something that made his comrades laugh, and Susie left with Violet. No one but Fargo saw Susie relieve the man of his sidearm and slip it into her pocket before she sauntered off. Fargo was duly impressed.

"Damn, Kitty," he whispered, "are all your girls professional pickpockets?"

She smiled. "We working girls have lots of skills, Skye. We have to."

"I reckon."

Fargo was also admiring the way Violet maneuvered herself around the smoke-filled room. Without giving the least sign that she was up to anything, she gathered her fellow females one by one, until they were all standing in a casual group behind the bar with Alfie. Although he couldn't see what was going on, Fargo knew Alfie was distributing weapons among them. Not that they needed them by this time, if they were all as adept at pilferage as Susie was.

Franklin seemed as oblivious to what the women were doing as the rest of the men in the saloon. He was deep into a conversation with a couple of his henchmen while Violet did her job, only looking up at one point when he reached for a glass that wasn't there. He lifted his head and bellowed, "Hey! Dammit, Amanda, I told you to bring me another glass of water!"

Amanda, busy behind the bar, turned and sang out in a cheerful voice that Fargo would have bet money she didn't

144

mean, "Coming, Mr. Franklin. I'll be right there." Her cheek still bore the imprint of Franklin's vicious slap.

Franklin grumbled something Fargo couldn't hear and resumed his conversation. A crash made Kitty jump. Fargo reached out a hand to steady her.

"My land, what was that?"

Fargo gestured at the room below. "I think one of Alfie's drinks just made its mark."

"Oh, yeah, I see." Kitty sounded pleased when she noticed what Fargo had pointed out. One of Franklin's men had slid off of his chair and fallen to the floor.

A man sitting at the same table peered at his fallen friend and said, "Cripes, Malcolm, what's the matter with you?"

Malcolm wasn't in any condition to respond. The man who'd asked the question didn't appear to be in much better shape himself. He tried to lean over his friend and swayed violently, grabbing the table to steady himself and shaking his head hard, reminding Fargo of a water-logged hound. He braced both of his hands on the table to keep himself upright in his chair.

"Good old Alfie," Kitty whispered.

Fargo agreed. "You about ready, Kitty? We're going to have to make our move any minute now."

He heard her suck in air and release it in a puff that lifted the dust from the floor. "I'm ready."

He nodded and continued to scan the room. One by one, with Violet leading them, the women sidled out from behind the bar and made their way to the stairs. They darted up the staircase one at a time, looking around to make sure no one noticed. Kitty silently rose to her feet—she'd taken her clunky shoes off—and pointed out each one's post as she arrived on the second-floor landing. The girls all shot curious glances at Fargo, but not one of them spoke. They were a well-disciplined group, and again Fargo was impressed.

He stood and had just pulled the lever on the Henry, when the door of the saloon opened. A blast of cold air whooshed into the room, dissipating some of the thick blue cigar smoke. He muttered, "Damn," and hoped it wasn't another bunch of Franklin hirelings.

It wasn't. Fargo's heart sank into his boots when he saw the hotel keeper, Mr. Purvis. Purvis was armed with what looked like a Brown Bess flintlock from the Revolution, and he pushed his way through the batwing doors, looking as nervous as a frightened cat. Mr. Gustavson was right behind him. At least the liveryman held a decent weapon. It looked like a Sharps to Fargo, although he didn't have a clear view of it. Mr. Dillard, the grocer, who stood next to Gustavson, was shaking like a leaf, thus rendering the Colt revolver in his hand practically useless.

"Oh, Lord, Skye, they didn't wait!" Kitty sounded bewildered.

"So I see," Fargo told her through gritted teeth.

"But you told them to wait until gunfire came from the saloon."

"Apparently they thought they knew better. Dammit, they're going to get themselves killed."

"Not to mention the girls and us."

With a quick jerk of his hand, Fargo signaled to the armed women in the upstairs hallway to prepare themselves. He'd hoped they'd have a clear shot of Franklin's men below, but now they were going to have to avoid hitting the three bumblers at the door, which would make their job harder.

"Franklin!"

It was Gustavson, who chunked a cartridge into his Sharps with a jerk of his hand on the lever.

"What's the matter with you, Gustavson?" Franklin sounded faintly annoyed. He gestured to a big man standing behind him, who quickly drew his weapon. He was fast, but Fargo was faster. Before the man could fire, he'd plugged him in the chest with a bullet from his Henry. Blood spurted from the wound onto Clay Franklin, who jumped up from his chair and shouted, "What the hell was that?"

"Get down!" Fargo shouted to Purvis, Gustavson, and Dillard. "Flat on the floor!"

Dillard, who wasn't cut out for this sort of thing, fainted dead away. Gustavson and Purvis turned to see where the shout had come from, making perfect targets of themselves. Fargo yelled to his crew of women, "Pick your targets and fire!" There wasn't going to be time for finesse, thanks to the citizens of Spanish Bend, who, too late, were attempting to defend their town.

It didn't take Franklin's men—the ones who were still awake and standing—anywhere near as long to understand what was happening as it did Gustavson and Purvis, although they didn't seem clear on where to shoot first. Purvis cried out in pain as a slug from someone's gun hit him in the upper arm. The sound galvanized him and Gustavson, though, and they dropped to the floor at last. Gustavson had the sense to upend a table and scramble behind it. He dragged Purvis, still clutching his arm, behind the table too, then crawled out, got hold of Dillard's foot, and towed him to shelter.

Fargo was glad to see the men take cover, but he didn't have time to fully appreciate their good sense, because hell and hot lead was breaking loose down below. Fargo and his team of female sharpshooters had the advantage over Franklin's men, because they were above them and had a fair view of the entire saloon.

Their visual advantage didn't last long. Soon, black smoke from the various guns filled the air and it became more difficult to see anything clearly. By that time, clarity of vision didn't matter too much since, except for Gustavson, Purvis, and Dillard lying on the floor beside the front door, there wasn't a man in the room whom Fargo didn't want dead. Except Alfie, of course, but he was behind the bar with his own weapon, taking well-aimed potshots into the crowd of scoundrels.

Fargo didn't know how long the battle of the Pecos Belle Saloon lasted, but it seemed like forever. The sound of shouts and screams from the women, yells and curses from the men, and gunfire from dozens of weapons nearly deafened him. When at last the shooting tapered off and the smoke was so thick he could scarcely draw breath, he heard Alfie's voice lift from the bar area.

"Skye! I think it's all over!"

Various voices from the murky room cried out their willingness to stop the mayhem and give up their weapons. A few groans and whimpers joined them in a feeble chorus. Several colorful curses floated up from men lying on the floor in pain.

"Stay down, Alfie. Don't take any chances." Fargo couldn't see a damned thing for all the smoke. He could barely hear, for that matter, over the ringing in his ears. Nevertheless, he called out to his troops, "Stop firing, girls, and don't move from your positions. We'll let Alfie reconnoiter and see what kind of damage we've done."

The women all obeyed at once. Fargo had seldom seen a better disciplined group than the girls of the Pecos Belle. He'd known generals who'd be ecstatic if their own soldiers obeyed orders so readily. He was proud of them.

The silence that followed the battle was nearly as loud as the gunfire had been. It seemed to stretch out until Fargo's nerves wanted to crawl out of his skin. After what seemed like an hour or two, he saw Gustavson, his big head looking fuzzy through the smoke and haze, peek around the table behind which he, Dillard, and Purvis were hiding.

"Be careful, Gustavson. Don't show yourself. We don't know what's going on down there."

The head vanished more quickly than it had appeared, but no more gunfire erupted. Maybe the battle truly was over for good. Fargo wasn't going to take any chances with the lives of Kitty's girls. He called, "Alfie, what's going on down there?"

"Not a thing, Skye. I'm collectin' weapons. Nobody's objected so far."

Fargo grinned as he saw Alfie slithering on his belly across the floor toward Franklin's table. He stopped grinning when Alfie's voice sailed up to him again.

"Dammit, Skye, I got me a sack full of guns, but Franklin's gone!"

"Gone?" Kitty stood up fast. "Where the hell did he go?"

"Open the damned door, Gustavson," Fargo called. "We can't see anything through the smoke."

He heard a scuttling sound, and the whoosh of the batwing doors being thrown open. Gustavson turned the knob on the heavy wooden door that kept the cold weather out, and a swirl of snow came inside on a blast of fresh, frigid air.

"Franklin's gone," Alfie announced, sounding crabby

about it. "And so's the two men who were guarding him. They snuck out the back door, I reckon."

"Well, hell." Fargo stood and motioned to Kitty's girls that they could get up from the floor. Now that the outdoor air had started blowing into the room below, he could see men lying on the floor. The ones who were conscious were belly-down and had their hands pressed to the backs of their heads. He nodded to Violet and Susie. There was lots of blood down there too, and he hoped none of the girls possessed queasy dispositions. "Go tie up the ones who aren't dead, girls, and bandage up the wounded. We'll load 'em on a wagon and ride them out of town after we figure out where Franklin went."

"He's probably headed out of town too," Alfie said.

"Dammit, he's the one I wanted most." Kitty stamped her foot.

Fargo smiled at her. "Don't worry, Kitty. Even if he gets away, he can't come back. He's got no soldiers left in town, and without him ordering things, the ones in the outlying ranches won't stick around for long."

"We won't let him come back. I'll send some fellows out to the ranches to let them know what happened." That declaration came from Gustavson, who was working down below. Fargo couldn't see what he was doing at first. Then he heard a rip and realized the liveryman was tearing the shirt off of one of Franklin's fallen hired guns. He still didn't know what Gustavson aimed to do with the shirt until he saw him rend it into strips and head for Purvis, who still held a hand to his sluggishly bleeding arm.

Suddenly, a shriek from outside ripped through the smoky atmosphere of the Pecos Belle Saloon. Everyone froze in shock.

A few seconds later Gustavson's voice came, and it shook. "That's Ursula."

"Oh, God." Kitty pressed a hand over her mouth.

Somebody kicked the door and the batwings flew inward. Silhouetted against the snowy night was Franklin, flanked by his two armed companions. In Franklin's arms was the struggling Ursula, Franklin's hand clamped over her mouth, her blue eyes huge with terror and hate.

14

"I'm leaving Spanish Bend," Franklin announced. "And you're not going to stop me, Fargo. I've got the insurance right here." He tightened his grip on the girl in his arms, provoking a stifled cry from her. He was likely to smother her if he kept that up.

"Don't hurt her." Gustavson's voice trembled as if the gale outside was blowing it. "You've done enough to her already."

"I won't hurt her, you fool. She's my ticket out of this damned dump. Who's with me?" His head whipped from side to side and scanned the room. Fargo presumed he was looking for any of his men who might be functional. Although a few of them lifted their heads from the floor to see what was going on, none of them tried to rise and rush to their leader's rescue.

Out of the corner of his eye, Fargo could see Alfie and Violet slip out the door Franklin himself had used to escape the battle only minutes earlier.

He lowered his Henry to his side. "I won't try to stop you, Franklin. Take the girl and get out of here."

"No!" Gustavson yelled. "Once he gets out of town, he won't need her any longer and he'll kill her and throw her away like trash."

"I won't kill her," Franklin lied. "I'll set her down at

the bend in the Pecos, and you can pick her up in an hour or so."

"Let him go, Gustavson," Fargo said calmly. "She'll be all right."

Gustavson spun around and shook a fist at Fargo. "You don't know him! He'll kill her, just like he killed her mother!"

"He's right, Skye," Kitty muttered at Fargo's side.

"It'll be all right, Kitty. You'll see," Fargo replied.

"Sure, it'll be all right," Franklin said with a sneer. "I'll keep my word."

"If you do, it'll be the first time," Kitty seethed, mad as a wet hen.

Fargo said, "Shhh, Kitty."

"Dammit, Skye, I won't be quiet! He'll hurt that girl!"

Fargo rolled his eyes and nudged her shoulder. "Please, Kitty, be quiet. Can't you trust me for another little while?"

"I *do* trust you! It's Franklin I don't trust!"

Kitty was glaring up at him. She wasn't looking, as Fargo was, at the snow-covered road behind Franklin and his men. She couldn't see Alfie and Violet, followed by an armed mob of women and children, walking silently through the snow to stand behind Franklin, their weapons ready and aimed.

Alfie and Violet pulled their triggers at the same time, causing a din as loud as a cannon blast. The men standing beside Franklin crumpled, and the band of townsfolk charged at Franklin's back. Franklin himself let out a startled "What the—?" before he was rammed by the mob and stumbled forward.

It was enough. His grip on Ursula Gustavson loosened for a split second, and her white teeth chomped down hard on his hand. He yelled in pain and shoved her into the saloon. As she stumbled away from him, his gun hand lifted.

Gustavson hollered, "No!"

Kitty shrieked, "Skye!"

Fargo heard neither of them. He had his Henry up and had let off a shot in less time than it took to blink. A red spot bloomed between Franklin's eyes, and his face registered an expression of stunned incredulity that lasted about three seconds. Then his expression went blank, his reptilian eyes rolled upward, and he fell face-first onto the floor of the Pecos Belle Saloon. A thin trickle of blood seeped from the wound.

Ursula stood staring at Franklin's body for a very few seconds before she let out a harsh sob and ran to her father, who closed his arms around her like pincers. Violet and Alfie stood at the door of the saloon, staring at the men they'd shot. Violet looked shaky, and Alfie put an arm around her to steady her. The band of townsfolk, some armed only with broomsticks and clubs, charged into the room.

Violet, watching in shock, started to cry. Alfie squeezed her shoulder and patted her gently, like a father comforting a daughter.

"It's all right, Violet. You had to do it. And those folks have been storing up their hate for a long time. Ever since Franklin and his men came to town."

"I know it," the girl said, her words muffled behind the hands she held over her mouth in dismay. "I just never shot nobody before—and today I shot two men." She pulled away and peeked at her handiwork through her fingers. Then her hands fell to her sides. Her back straightened. She grinned, "I did all right, didn't I, Alfie?"

Fargo and Kitty laughed.

"You did damned good, Violet," Alfie told her.

The girls of the Pecos Belle Saloon cheered as they watched the citizens of Spanish Bend surround the men who'd made their lives miserable for so many months.

It took a while for Skye, Kitty, Alfie, Kitty's girls, and the citizens of Spanish Bend to finish cleaning up the remnants of Clay Franklin's band of ruffians. Once the townsfolks got through sorting everything out, they hauled the corpses off to the undertaker's. The undertaker, a Mr. Stone, didn't look as happy about the bounty before him as Fargo thought he should—they'd certainly given him plenty of business.

After they'd removed the dead men, they bound each living man hand and foot and began loading them into Mr. Gustavson's wagon. They didn't all fit, so another wagon had to be commissioned from Mr. Dillard, who awoke from his faint after Violet dumped a bucket of cold water on him.

Kitty stood back, dusted off her hands, and stared at the men crammed into the two wagons like buzzards on a carcass. "Where are you going to take them, Skye?"

"Alfie and Gustavson are going to drive them to Fort Sumner. It'll take a day or so to get there, explain things, and get back again."

The remnants of Franklin's band of ruffians stared sullenly at them from the wagon beds. One of them cried out, "This ain't fair, Fargo! We ain't even armed. Besides, it's cold, and we're liable to freeze to death on the trip to Fort Sumner."

"You should have thought of that before you tried to take over our town," Kitty said.

The man muttered, "Bitch."

Kitty marched up to him and slapped his face. "If you want to get there alive, you'd better shut up."

The man said no more.

Kitty seemed satisfied. She nodded decisively. "I reckon the army will know what to do with them."

Fargo shrugged. "Even if they don't, I don't think any of these men will cause you any more trouble. Without Franklin to organize them, they'll probably scatter and take up jobs with other people. Some of them might even find something useful to do for a change."

"I doubt it." Kitty sniffed.

"You're probably right."

"Did Gustavson tell you he's writing a letter to the territorial governor?"

"Yeah. Until they send a marshal, Gustavson and Purvis are holding down the sheriff's job. They'll do all right together."

"I suppose so." Kitty shook her head and looked sad. "I hope that poor little girl will be all right."

"Ursula?" Fargo glanced from the wagon full of hardcases to Gustavson's Livery Stable. He could see Ursula Gustavson from where he stood. She was timidly peeking out from behind a wooden pillar. "I don't know, Kitty. She's been through an awful lot."

"Don't I know it." She frowned at the men in the wagon. "I wish I could treat some of these men the way they treated her."

"Life isn't fair sometimes, especially to women."

"You can say that again."

Something occurred to him, and he asked, "Say, Kitty, do you suppose Violet could take charge of Ursula while her daddy's gone? It might be good for both of them."

Kitty's eyes opened wide, and her smile was brilliant. "Skye Fargo, if you aren't the smartest man on earth, I don't know who is." She gestured Violet over and asked her if she'd be willing to help keep Ursula company during these trying times. Violet, whose heart was as big as she was small, agreed readily.

Fargo and Kitty watched as she walked over to the girl, leaned close, and spoke softly to her. Ursula looked uncertain for a minute, then nodded. Violet turned her head, smiled at Fargo and Kitty, took Ursula's hand, and walked into the livery stable with the ragged blond girl.

Kitty sniffled at his side, and Fargo looked down in surprise. "Are you crying, Kitty O'Malley?"

"Hell, no," she lied, and sniffled again.

He gave her a hug.

"We're ready, Skye, if that's the last of them," said Alfie, who looked happier than Fargo had seen him since he arrived in Spanish Bend.

"That's the last of them, all right."

Alfie glanced at Kitty. "Will you be all right while I'm gone, Kitty?"

She hugged him hard. "Of course, I will, Alfie. Skye'll take care of me."

"He'd better." Alfie smiled as he said it and shook Fargo's hand.

Fargo gave Alfie a leg up, and the older man climbed into the driver's seat. He'd already laid out a blanket to sit on, and as he wrapped another one over his shoulders, he took the reins and got ready to release the brake.

"Take care of yourself, Alfie," Kitty said. She blew him a kiss.

"I will, sweetie." They could scarcely hear him for all the woolen scarves and mufflers he had wrapped around his head and mouth.

Gustavson got into the second wagon. "We'll be back as soon as we can." He cast a worried peek at his livery stable, then looked straight at Kitty. "Will you watch her for me, Miss Kitty? I know watching kids ain't generally in your line, but I'd surely appreciate it."

"You'd be surprised," Kitty told him dryly. "Anyway, it's already taken care of, Mr. Gustavson. Violet took Ursula under her wing. They'll be good for each other."

Gustavson blinked, surprised, then nodded. "Thank you, Miss Kitty. You're a kind woman."

Kitty looked uncomfortable with the praise. She glanced at Alfie. "You watch out for yourself and Alfie, you hear me?"

Gustavson tipped his hat, settled it firmly on his head, and tied it down with a woolen scarf.

The frigid wind howled like a pack of wolves, but Alfie claimed his old joints hadn't predicted any further snow for a couple of days at the least. And, while Skye Fargo wasn't old enough to predict the weather by his joints just yet, his frontier instincts told him Alfie was right. It would be as cold as a son of a bitch, though, and he wished the two men were back from their journey instead of beginning it. But it wouldn't take them long, and they'd have several armed men from Spanish Bend riding along to assure their safety to the fort and back.

After lifting his swaddled arm once more in a farewell salute, Alfie clicked to the mules and he rumbled off, Gustavson's wagon right beside him. The armed outriders shrugged against the wind and moved slowly alongside the two wagons.

Fargo saw snow in the air churned up by the wagon wheels and shook his head. "This territory has the hardest weather and geography I've ever seen."

"Does it?" Kitty didn't seem to notice. She waved after Alfie until her arm got tired.

She turned to Fargo and shrugged. "I'm not interested in the weather, Skye."

He peered down at her. "No? What are you interested in?"

"Guess." She laughed, grabbed his arm, and tugged him toward the saloon.

Amanda skipped up to them and stopped right in front of the Trailsman. "Mr. Fargo, I think it's time you gave Kitty a rest and met some of the rest of us."

He blinked down at her. "You do?"

Amanda grinned at Kitty. "You've already sampled his wares, Kitty. It's our turn now."

"What's this 'our turn' business?" Skye was getting worried.

Kitty lifted her eyebrows in a mock show of puritanical outrage. "I've never been so shocked in my life."

Amanda giggled. "Not for a long time, I'll bet. But it really is our turn now, Kitty. Don't we deserve it after all we did?"

Putting her hands on her hips, Kitty grinned. "Well, shoot, I reckon I can't argue with that logic, Amanda. Besides"—she turned to glance at the livery stable, where Ursula and Violet had entered—"I reckon I have to do a neighbor a good turn." She turned back to Amanda and gave her a broad wink. "Take good care of him, Amanda."

"Don't you worry about that." Amanda's hand took over from where Kitty's had left Skye Fargo's arm, and she steered him along toward the saloon. Susie, Julie, and two other girls joined them. "Looks like you've got your afternoon's work cut out for you, Mr. Fargo."

Fargo's gaze went from one pretty woman to the other to the other and he sighed deeply. "I'll do my best."

Life could get lots worse.

LOOKING FORWARD!
The following is the opening
section from the next novel in the exciting
Trailsman **series from Signet:**

THE TRAILSMAN #219
ARIZONA SILVER STRIKE

Arizona, 1860, where the promise of the
mother lode wafts sweet in the desert air,
mingling with the scents of spilled blood
and burnt powder . . .

"I said, get down the shaft!"

The girl put her two fisted-hands on her hips. "Daddy, you're going to have to stop acting like I'm seven! I can shoot, you know! Whoever's out there, I can sink a lead ball between his—"

"*Now*, Clementine!" he roared, and the girl, twenty-two years old and just as stubborn and strong-willed as her mother had been, rolled her eyes a last time.

She retreated into the mine's mouth with a "Hmph!" just as a slug sang off the rock face beside him. Tell McBride ducked, but as he did, he noticed that his daughter picked up a little speed.

Good, he thought with a smile, then turned to business. Tell called out to his brother, Tyrone, who was hunkered down behind a careless pile of boulders, his eye fairly glued to the sites of his long gun. "You see him?"

"No, dammit!" Tyrone replied, lifting his gaze from the sites only long enough to spit out a brown stream of tobacco juice. "He were just down there, by the water-hole, in that clump of paloverde. Got half a mind to just start pepperin' it again."

"Not unless you got as good a nose for lead as you do for silver," Tell warned. "We ain't got but six slugs left between us, and no more to melt and mold till we go to town again."

Tell knelt beside his brother, and they both searched the brush, looking for the smallest signs of motion. "Don't know why you had to take a potshot at that feller, anyhow, Tyrone," he said, disgusted. "Probably would'a just watered that fancy horse a'his and moved on, and never would'a knowed we was here! Six slugs ain't gonna do us no good if we're beset by Apaches."

Tyrone growled something under his breath that Tell didn't quite catch, although it was likely something about younger brothers being seen and not heard—even if that brother was only two summers younger and fifty-three years old. Between an uppity daughter and a bossy older brother turning him this way and that, fairly banging him over the head with words, Tell figured it was a pure miracle they hadn't driven him into the ground like a corkscrew.

"There!" hissed Tyrone, shifting the barrel of his long gun slightly and pointing. "Reckon I should chance a shot?"

"All of a sudden you're askin' me?" By this time, Tell had taken up his old flintlock. Tyrone always sneered at it, called it fit for nothing but the trash heap, but it had been their daddy's. It had served him well enough during the War of 1812, and Tell didn't have any reason to believe it wouldn't continue to take care of him and his own.

Tyrone scowled. "Well, you're the one complainin' about the lead shortage. Ain't seen a single Apache the whole dang time we been working this diggin', anyhow." He paused, squinting along the barrel. "Crikey! He ain't fired but that one time, and I can't even see his horse no more! Now, how can a whole, big, loud-colored horse just disappear? What'd he do? Put it down a gopher hole?"

"Close, but no cigar."

Both men wheeled at the new voice, which came from the rise at their backs. Someone stood on the slope above the mine shaft: a tall man, lank, and with a close-cropped beard. A Henry rifle glinted dully in his hands, and by the look of him, he could probably do quite a bit of damage with or without it. He looked more annoyed than mad, which promised to be, so far as Tell was concerned, a blessing.

The man shook his head, and said, "You boys want to lay down those arms and tell me just why the hell you were shooting at me?"

Once he'd collected the men's firearms and ascertained they were the only souls in camp, Skye Fargo whistled for the Ovaro. The horse, a tall and well-made black-and-white paint, rose from behind a clump of mesquite, shook the dust from his gleaming hide, and moseyed toward them.

"Crikey," breathed one of the old codgers. "Dang horse does tricks."

They were a couple of rock-breakers, by the look of them. Dust lay thick on their trousers, shirts, and boots and had worked into their creased faces, as if they spent their days and nights burrowing underground. Their picks and shovels and other equipment—if such existed—were hidden away, but Fargo didn't care to snoop for them. If, indeed, there was a mine, it was their business. He just didn't like people taking potshots at him.

He leaned his Henry against a rock and crossed his arms. "You boys got names?" he asked.

"Puddin' Tame," said the taller of the two. "Ask me again and I'll tell you the same."

The other one rolled his eyes. "I'm Tell McBride, and this here smart apple would be my brother, Tyrone. And who might you be?"

"Name's Fargo," he said, extending his hand. "Skye Fargo."

He'd already decided these boys weren't the type to kill. They'd just got a little nervous, that was all. Living alone in the desert could do that to a fellow.

Tell took his outstretched hand and gave it a firm shake. "Say, I believe I've heard'a you! You the one they call the Trailsman?"

Fargo nodded. "Guilty. I'm on my way to Jupiter. September Downy asked me to mail a letter for him."

Tyrone, who still hadn't shaken his hand, arched a brow. "You say you're a friend of Sept's?"

Fargo nodded. "His place is a far piece from nowhere and anywhere. Been riding three days and haven't seen fresh water since the Flatheads. Sorry if that spring down there is private property. I had no intention to trespass."

Tyrone, his face still wadded into a scowl, said, "Well, Jupiter's just a hop, skip, and a jump down the road. You can make 'er in three hours if you leave now."

"Uncle Tyrone!" said a new—and distinctly female—voice. "Where are your manners?"

All three men turned toward the far edge of the boulders, and there stood the prettiest girl Skye Fargo had seen in a month of Sundays.

Glossy hair so dark brown it was nearly black was pulled back at the nape of her neck, and shorter strands waved around her face like fairy curls. Her face, even-featured with long-lashed, pale blue eyes, was tanned to gold by the sun.

She was lush of breast and hip and slim of waist, and her long legs were clad in trousers which were considerably cleaner—and considerably better filled out—than those of her Uncle Tyrone. Her full bosom strained against the bone buttons of the man's shirt she wore.

"Gol-dang it, Clementine!" Tell said, and slapped his leg with his floppy hat, exposing a bald head fringed with curly salt-and-pepper hair. "It thought I told you to stay hid until we saw what was what!"

She cocked her head. "I thought you already knew that, Daddy," she said with a smile aimed at nobody but Fargo.

He smiled back. She was like a rose grown up in a briar patch.

"We have a guest," she continued, "and a famous one, too, if I'm to listen to you. Mr. Fargo, I should like to apologize for my father and my uncle. Not only was it rude to shoot at you, but we can scarcely afford the expenditure of ammunition. Would you care to join us for a cup of coffee?"

"Crikey!" exclaimed Tyrone in obvious exasperation. "Why did you ever send her to Boston-town for anyhow, Tell?"

"Beats the holy pee-waddin' out of me," Tell muttered as they all obediently trouped along behind Clementine, down into a hollow hidden from view of the rocks and the spring, where the brothers had made their campsite.

All the way down, Fargo was watching Clementine's little backside swish back and forth in those pants.

Tempting. Very tempting.